'Anyone sitting by his fireside with an A. J. Alan volume is ensured a delightful evening. His is no book for a deck-chair on a beach, a hammock and a sunny day. Though laughter is plentiful, the supernatural hovers persistently; a skeleton is liable to pop its head out of the cupboard and mar the feast of mirth. But, Alan being the spellbinder he is, after pushing a corpse under your nose—a murdered corpse, sometimes a putrefying one—he will characteristically square the circle with politely insincere apologies for having curdled your blood.'

But That's a Detail

Collected stories of A. J. Alan

Edited by Dave Morris

Spark Furnace Books

Published 2012 by Spark Furnace Books,
an imprint of Fabled Lands LLP
www.sparkfurnace.com

ISBN 978-1478268413

BUT THAT'S A DETAIL

CONTENTS

INTRODUCTION

A J Alan was the pseudonym of Leslie Harrison Lambert, a Foreign Office official, amateur magician, former Royal Navy officer and cryptographer in Hut 3 (the Enigma team) at Bletchley Park. Phew. Well, why did he need a pseudonym, you'd like to know, and the answer to that is that he made occasional broadcasts on the wireless in the '20s and '30s, spinning tall tales that he wrote himself and pasted onto large squares of cardboard so as not to disturb the audience with the sound of rustling pages. Lambert — that is, Alan — always turned up at the BBC in full evening dress, and with his own candle and matches as contingency in the event of a studio light failing.

Now the reason I'm telling you all this is that I was introduced to Mr Alan's — I mean, Mr Lambert's— stories many years ago by my friend William Burton, who was read them by his housemaster at school who might very well have been one of Alan's original listeners. The stories made a strong impression on me. They are shaggy dog tales for the most part, often but not always steering away at the last moment from anything as vulgar as mere plot resolution. Some have a delicate touch of the supernatural about them, though only in the way a chap might tell you about an actual spooky experience, nothing so overtly supernatural as in an M R James tale. In the most part the stories are very effective at doing just what the storyteller intended, namely letting you pass an agreeable quarter of an hour in the company of an amusing raconteur who's spinning an elegant verbal picture of how he went gadding about on various *outré* and/or outrageous adventures. All of them are charming and whimsical, and deserve a place along Dunsany's tales of Jorkens as the most sparkling literary *écume*.

Anyway, it turns out that A J Alan breathed his last in a Norfolk guest house a tad over seventy years ago. Which I'm sure was quite a tragedy, especially for Mrs Alan (well, Mrs Lambert, of course, is who I mean) who followed her husband soon after, poor woman. But time heals all wounds, and the silver lining in this case is that the stories are now in the public domain. Here's a fine body of work which no longer need languish, secured by the strangling chain of copyright. Getting on for a century after he first leaned close to the microphone and said, 'Good evening, everyone' (which was in 1924, but that's a detail), A J Alan's *oeuvre* can enjoy a new lease of life.

Dave Morris
Wandsworth, 2011

PREFACE

GOOD EVENING, everyone (or good morning, after-noon or night, as the case may be).

I wanted to put this preface in the middle or at the end of this book, the idea being that someone might come across it and read it, but the publishers object-ed. They said it wouldn't be a preface unless it came at the beginning, and Mr. Hutchinson looked so wistful about it that I had to give way, so here we are.

First of all, I should like to express my gratitude to Sir John Reith and the staff of the B.B.C. for all the courtesy and assistance I have received from them during the last four years—they have always been most helpful.

I should also like to take this opportunity of thanking the large number of listeners who have written me such charming and appreciative letters. They have given me no end of encouragement.

As regards the stories themselves—everything I say over the microphone is taken down in shorthand and transcribed afterwards, and when the idea of publishing my experiences was mooted I began to try to turn them into something like English. However, after a glance at my first efforts in this direction, Messrs. Hutchinsons called loudly for the transcript of the shorthand notes, and insisted on using it instead. You must, therefore, blame them and not me if any of the expressions in this book seem to verge upon the colloquial.

A. J. Alan, January, 1928.

The 19 Club

I BELONG to a dining club – as a matter of fact I'm the secretary – but apart from that there's nothing much to distinguish it from lots of other clubs of a similar kind.

It's called the 19 Club.

You may think that sounds rather mysterious, but it isn't in the least, really. There are 19 members and it was started in 1919, so I don't honestly see how it could have been called anything else.

We are just a lot of people who had a certain job to do during the war, and when it was over we thought it would be rather fun for us all to meet and have dinner together every now and then. So we do, twice a year: on June the first and December the first. When the date falls on a Sunday we make it the Monday.

This arrangement saves the secretary a lot of work, as there aren't any notices to send out – in fact being a secretary is no trouble at all. We always stick to the same restaurant and I go in two or three days before and order the dinner. When it's over, just before we leave, I go round and collect thirty bob or so from everyone and hand it straight over to the head-waiter; he gives me a receipt, which I generally lose, and there you are.

Nothing could possibly be simpler from my point of view, or, you'd think, from anyone else's, but it was this very simplicity which nearly landed us in a mess on June the first this year.

If you'll examine our somewhat casual procedure for a moment, you'll see that it leaves the management of the restaurant, and of course the waiters, quite in the dark as to who any of us are (not that we care): for all they know is that we are the "19 Club", and they write it up on a card down in the hall. There's a highly polished mahogany board on an easel just inside the entrance, giving the names of the rooms – and they shove it on that.

Well, by some mischance, a prowling journalist in search of prey wandered into the hall during our last December meeting, and he happened to see this card.

He asked who we were and the people down below couldn't tell him because they didn't know – they said they had no information about us of any kind. This appears to have piqued his curiosity, and he promptly sent up his card addressed to the secretary asking for an immediate interview.

A waiter brought it to me during quite an amusing speech that was going on, and I thought it was rather cheek. I just said "No", or words to that effect, and would Mr. Heacham please go away – Heacham was the name on the card. I mean, the freedom of the Press is all very well in its way, but if a few friends can't dine together quietly without reporters butting in – well, it's a bit too thick. However, Mr. Heacham did not go away. He seems to have hung about outside for the rest of the evening until we left, and then got the commissionaire at the door to point me out to him. I never saw him at all, but he must have followed me home and then looked up my name in the directory, because two days later there was a letter from him – he wrote from some office in the Strand.

He described himself as a free-lance journalist and said that he'd been commissioned by the editor of a well-known London Daily to write a series of articles on dining clubs. Mind you, I never believe this story because I think it's so much more likely that they write the articles first and hawk them round to the editors afterwards – but I may be wrong. He went on to ask for the names of all our members, together with any biographical details likely to interest the public, and so on. I believe he added that it would be a fine advertisement for us. At any rate I called loudly for my stylographic pen and wrote him a letter to which he made no reply – and there it was. But it only goes to show that some people don't like you to mind your own business.

By the bye, I made a statement a minute or two ago which, I'm afraid, wasn't strictly accurate: I said that when this man's card was brought to me at the dinner, there was a speech going on. Well, actually, we don't have speeches in the generally accepted sense of the term – what merely happens is this. Supposing anyone does something clever or interesting, like flying to Australia and back or motoring across China or inventing something wonderful, we ask him to come and dine, and then afterwards he just gets up and spouts about it – er, describes his achievement in an informal kind of way.

And we don't confine ourselves to respectable exploits either. If anyone were to break into the Bank of England and get away with a million pounds, I'm quite sure we should ask him to come and tell us exactly how he did it. So you can see that in one way and another we do get a good deal of amusement and instruction, but we don't attempt to get it for nothing. Oh no: there's an honorarium of ten guineas which we always hope the guest of the evening will accept, and we are getting more and more sanguine about its getting accepted, because no one's ever refused it yet.

You'd be surprised at some of the distinguished people to whom a tenner hasn't come amiss: in fact the man who pouched my furtive envelope with the greatest gusto was a certain Chancellor of the Exchequer – I shan't say who it was. He'd come along and explained his budget to us.

It isn't anyone's job in particular to procure these artists, but we all keep our eyes open for suitable "turns."

At all events, last March I happened to come across a paragraph in the newspaper. It was tucked away in a corner but it took my fancy very much. It was all about an Englishman called Kennedy who'd escaped from a foreign prison. There's apparently a small island off the coast of Java which the Dutch use as a convict settlement, and Kennedy was there serving a sentence of ten years.

Well, whether they weren't kind to him, or he'd got tired of the place, I don't know, but one fine morning he decided to leave. He climbed over the barbed wire when no one was looking and made straight for the house of the Governor of the island.

The Governor wasn't in, so Master Kennedy went into his bedroom, put on one of his uniforms and strolled down to the harbour. There he borrowed the Governor's motor-boat and left the island flying the Governor's flag. He even managed to extract a salute from one of our light cruisers which was lying in the harbour at the time.

After that all trace of him was lost. I showed this paragraph to several other members of the 19 Club, and they all agreed that he was just the lad for us if only we could get hold of him.

It so happened that I knew the editor of the paper which had published the report, and I went round and asked him to let me know if he ever heard anything more. He promised to make enquiries, but he wasn't very hopeful.

However, roughly seven weeks later I got a somewhat cryptic letter from a man in Chiswick. He said he was just back from the East and understood that I'd been enquiring about a certain person whose name began with K. If I still wanted the information would I please call at the address on his letter (No. 23 something-or-other Gardens) and ask for John Smith. This I did that same afternoon. Something-or-other Gardens (and I'm not going to give the name) consisted entirely of red-brick villas with "Apartments to Let" in the windows. The door was opened to me by an obvious landlady – quite a nice old thing – and when I asked for John Smith she somehow looked as though she knew it was an assumed name. She said he was expecting me, but would I mind not stopping too long as he'd been ill. I promised not to, of course, and then she showed me into the right-hand front sitting-room.

It was typically, but comfortably, furnished. There I found a nervous little rabbit of a man of about thirty-five who kept darting to the window and peering out into the street. He also had one of those high voices which have never broken – it was so pronounced that it was quite difficult to get used to. We discussed the weather until the landlady got tired of listening at the door, and he admitted what I'd already guessed, and you too, probably, that he wasn't John Smith at all but John Kennedy, the escaped convict himself. He apologised for receiving me in such a hole-and-corner way but he was terrified of the police finding him and banding him over to the Dutch. I said they'd get no help from me, and we finally got down to the business of the 19 Club dinner.

He was a bit chary at first of coming out into th
open so much, but he eventually thought he'd risk i
and he brightened up quite a lot at the idea of
tenner. The only trouble was that he was what the
call "a bit pushed for the stuff" and he only had th
clothes he stood up in. Could anything be done in th
way of an advance? He was quite frank about hi
affairs: he'd had a bad go of flu soon after landin
which had left him with a flabby heart muscle an
prevented him from looking for a job; he was in deb
to his landlady, and altogether things weren't to
rosy. Anyway, I was able to let him have enough t
square his landlady and get some clothes, and I als
told him I'd get the Club to spring a bit more in th
way of fee. I was most careful not to refer to his priso
experiences because he didn't seem up to it, so I gav
him the time and place of the dinner and came awa
My only regret was that his voice was so singularl
unsuitable for the recital of daring deeds.

It would be as well, perhaps, to explain that to ge
to the room we dine in at the restaurant you have t
go through a sort of ante-room, and it is our custom
to assemble first of all for sherry and cocktails in thi
smaller room.

Well, on June the first we were all waiting in thi
room when John Smith walked in. (We'd arranged t
go on calling him that in his own interest.)

He looked a good deal better in health than whe
I'd seen him last, but he'd evidently been fortifying
himself against the ordeal of delivering his discours
Not that he was at all screwed, but he had undoub
edly had one or two. It was a good thing he was a bi
late and that there was only time for him to have on
glass of sherry before we went in. I also took th
precaution of sitting next to him and seeing that h

didn't overdo it. It seemed mean, but it was no use him getting tight too soon.

Anyway, dinner went off all right, and soon after "the King", when the waiters had all cleared out, our chairman invited him to tell us about his experiences out East. He also gave an assurance on behalf of the Club that nothing he said would go any further. Whereupon John Smith Kennedy got up and proceeded to tell his story, and a very astonishing story it was.

He led off by saying that the crime of which he'd been convicted had been a burglary in Brussels, of all places.

No one said anything, but most of us thought it rather peculiar for a man to be sent to a Dutch penal settlement for an offence, however heinous, against the laws of Belgium. He made other equally glaring mistakes too, and it soon became perfectly clear that the whole story was a pack of lies from beginning to end and that he'd never been nearer Java than Southend.

Things got so ridiculous that it was finally put to him that he was romancing – and he admitted it without any beating about the bush. He said lie wasn't the man Kennedy at all, that he'd never been in prison, and that the whole thing was a hoax. We said, "Ha, ha, very funny and all that, but if you aren't Kennedy, who are you?"

And then he sprang his great surprise.

You remember that man Heacham, the journalist who'd sent up his card and tried to find out about the Club? Well – he was Heacham, getting a bit of his own back. I didn't see at first how he'd got hold of the Kennedy story in connection with us, but he explained with fiendish glee that he occasionally did work for my editor man, and he'd actually been sent for and given the job of making enquiries about it.

The editor must have mentioned my name and told him why I wanted the information. Needless to say he hadn't traced Kennedy, but he'd used the circumstances to score off me and the Club – and there was no denying that he'd done it jolly well. We shouldn't have cared two hoots if lie hadn't been so beastly offensive: he strutted up and down and jeered at us and that wasn't the worst – he was going straight along to the Daily What Not and the whole story would be in the paper next morning, complete with such of our names as he knew. He got so truculent that if he hadn't been our guest I am quite sure someone would have slogged him on the beak. We told him that we didn't wish the story to appear in the paper and should take steps to prevent it, whereupon he completely lost his hair and got awfully excited. He said: "I'm still in the doctor's hands for my heart. If you offer me any violence it'll be the worse for you." It was pointed out to him that no one had the slightest intention of using any violence, and I can't make it too clear that nothing which any of us said or did could have been taken as in the least threatening.

We did, however, say that before we left we should like a few minutes to discuss the situation in private, and would he mind going into the anteroom.

He did, and one of us went with him to keep him company.

Well, the rest of us hadn't been talking, for more than a minute when the man who'd gone in with Heacham appeared at the door and said, "I wish you fellers would come and have a look at this bird. He doesn't seem very well."

So we all crowded in and – my word – he didn't look at all well. He'd fallen forward in a chair, apparently in a faint or fit or something.

One of our members was a doctor and he examined him for a moment, and then he said, "I'm sorry, good people, but this is a bad show. The man's dead", and he went on to explain how a heavy dinner and over-excitement had caused acute dilatation of the heart when it was a bit groggy, and it had snuffed out. Extremely simple, no doubt, from the medical point of view, but devilish awkward from ours.

We were very sorry, of course, but, at the same time, we couldn't help feeling a little annoyed with this person for coming to the dinner under false pretences and then going and dying on us as well, so there definitely wasn't the frantic amount of sympathy which there otherwise would have been. It would be bound to get into the papers, and a tragedy like that always does a restaurant a certain amount of harm, and it would also mean that some of us would have to spend a merry morning in the coroner's court.

So we were all standing about looking rather grave, and putting our cigars down, when one man remarked in a thoughtful kind of way: "What an awful lot of trouble it would have saved if only this individual could have survived long enough to get home." And then he gave a little nod – just like that; and, as everyone knows, a nod is sometimes as a good as a wink, especially when it comes from anyone as high up in the service as he was – and his meaning was so utterly scandalous that I'm sure all of you will have grasped it.

I asked him. I said: "Is it too late, sir, for you to get a game of bridge somewhere?" And he thought: No, it wasn't too late. He caught the eye of two or three more of similar rank to himself and they all sauntered out.

When they'd gone we put our heads together and settled our course of action.

We posted a man on the door to keep out stray waiters and went and fetched all the hats and coats, including the unfortunate Heacham's. While we were putting his on, the man with the largest car was told to go and get it and send his chauffeur home. As soon as word came through that it was at the door we got a move on.

A sort of advance guard of five went on ahead to make a demonstration. They were to send all available commissionaires for cars and taxis and generally clear the entrance of hotel staff. The main body, so to speak, followed a little way behind—this main body consisted of another man and me supporting Heacham, with the rest of the 19 Club in close formation all round us.

We went down the stairs without the slightest check, all laughing and talking, though not feeling a bit like it; but when we got into the hall we were confronted by a most appalling snag. They'd gone and rigged up the revolving doors. They'd been folded back out of the way before dinner, but I suppose it must have turned cooler during the evening. Anyway, there the brutes were revolving away like anything, and we wondered how on earth we were going to manage. Perhaps some of you've tried going through those doors two at once. It's a bit of a squash at the best of times, when you're both of you alive, but you try it when one of you isn't and you'll admit that it's no fun at all.

We couldn't stop and confer without attracting attention, so our front rank went through and formed a screen on the outside. Then, as secretary of the Club, I felt it my duty to be entirely responsible for our guest, and he gave me no help at all. When we were half-way through and completely shut off from the outer world, his hat fell off – I had to retrieve it with one hand and keep him propped up with the other. The people who were turning the doors round saw and backed water to give me time, but it was a trying experience and I'm quite prepared to swap nightmares with anyone. I didn't feel happy until we'd got him into the car, and even then "happy" is rather an over-statement. Another man and I sat with him between us at the back, and there was just the owner in front, driving. He drove very carefully, too, because it wouldn't have done for us to run into anything and all get asked for our names and addresses. Also, we didn't want to get to Chiswick too early. As it was, in spite of simply crawling the whole way, we found a light in the first floor window, so we kept straight on. We came back in ten minutes but it was still there, and we drove about the district for the best part of an hour, passing the house at intervals, before it was put out.

However, it finally was, and the last stage of our operations began.

The car dropped us and drove off to wait a few turnings away. The other man and I carried our friend up the garden path and in at the front door. This was easy because we'd got his key, but then we struck another bad patch. When I'd called at the house the first time there'd been linoleum on the hall floor, but this had evidently been taken up, leaving nothing but bare tiles. There wasn't even a mat, and when we stepped on to these tiles straight off a gravel path you can imagine the row we made – slate pencils weren't in it – and it woke the landlady.

She came to the top of the stairs and called down: "Is that Mr. Heacham?" and I said "Yes", in a very high voice (after all it was). Then she said "Your cocoa's on the kitchen stove", and I said, "Thanks very much. Good night", and she mercifully went back to bed.

We then breathed again and got Heacham into his room and switched on the light. We took off his hat and coat and arranged him as naturally as we could in an armchair. I went along to the kitchen and fetched his cocoa and cup and saucer and poured some out for him.

If we'd been his murderers, and we almost felt like it, we couldn't have taken more pains, but I should like to put it on record that from first to last he was treated with all due respect. We didn't forget to leave the light burning, and his own fingerprints were on the cup and saucer.

We got away without a sound, picked up the car as arranged and reached home without incident.

There wasn't an inquest, or if there was it didn't get into any paper, and everything must have passed off quite smoothly, but we had an anxious few days all the same.

We were anxious, because I'd made one foolish mistake, as, criminals so often do. On the face of it it was trifling, but even so it ought to have rotted up the whole of our good work.

I'd come away with Heacham's latchkey in my overcoat pocket.

A Joy Ride

AT THE BEGINNING of this last September I was spending a long weekend with some friends of mine who live near Ascot. He's a member of a big firm of underwriters. Not that it matters in the least what he does for a living, but I just mention it — and in case you don't know what an underwriter is you've only to look at the end of your insurance policy and you'll find a list of seven names applied with a rubber stamp. Those are underwriters, and they are the unfortunate individuals who have to fork out when you make a claim. Incidentally, I can't help thinking that on occasions like the fifth of November underwriters must feel rather overwrought. All the same, I must admit that my friend seems to thrive on taking these appalling risks.

I've called it a long weekend because I was staying till Tuesday morning.

Well — after we'd gone up to bed on the Monday night I saw a glare in the sky and actual smoke and flames appearing over some trees about half a mile off. I felt a bit of a brute but I went along to my host's room and said, "I hate to talk shop, but there's a perfectly good house on fire functioning quite close to. Don't you think something ought to be done about it?"

He came dashing back to my room and looked out of the window, and then he said, "Lor, that must be the Stimsons'. We shall have to go along and help." So we flung on some suitable garments and started off for this place.

It never does to go empty-handed to a fire in the country, so we took a ladder with us. By the time we arrived on the scene they'd given up trying to put the fire out as a bad job. There wasn't any water.

They were merely trying to save what furniture and so on they could. The lawn was already strewn with a somewhat embarrassing array of one thing and another, and as the staircases had both gone we propped up our ladder against a first floor window and carried on the good work till the roof fell in.

After that we left the various fire-brigades and took the inmates of the house back to our place and put them up as best we could. We all turned out of our rooms, but I don't think anyone actually went to bed.

There was a ghastly meal of sandwiches and coffee at about six, and after that I bagged a bathroom and got clean. Then, after breakfast, we went and inspected the ruins of the house, and such of us as had to came up to town.

I turned up at my office with the full intention of taking the afternoon off, but when I got there there was what they call a "flap" on; you know, a panic. It was about something quite futile — panics usually are — but it meant everyone staying till it was over. I didn't get home till after seven, by which time I was dead to the world. I don't know about you, but I simply cannot do without sleep indefinitely. It's all right for about thirty-six hours, but then I start dropping off at odd moments.

The trouble was that they were expecting me here at the B.B.C. at 10.15 to tell you about the 19 Club.

I changed and had a light dinner at home and slept solidly all the way to Savoy Hill. They were awfully good when I arrived — they plied me with strong black coffee up in the canteen and it kept me going just long enough to tell my story, and then I fell asleep in front of the microphone. Colonel Brand looked in and shook me, and said: "If you don't mind waiting a few minutes I'll give you a lift home." Apparently there was a party of people whom he was going to drop on the way, but they weren't quite ready to start. They were being shown the control-room first. Presently he came along with these people and we all piled into his car. It was bit of a squash as we were seven up, so I sat on the floor and leant back against the knees of some young woman. I'm sure she was delightful, but her knees were bony. They very nearly kept me awake.

The next thing I remember was our driving into the courtyard of Queen Anne's Mansions. There are several entrances to the flats round this courtyard and we stopped at the one in the middle of the right-hand side. We all got out and then there was a discussion. These good souls wanted us to go up to their flat and have a drink, and Colonel Brand said he would, and I was just beginning to say I was afraid I couldn't stop when the hall-porter chipped in and said the car couldn't stop where it was. If it was going to be left for any length of time it would have to be parked in the middle of the quad by the fountain.

So our five friends went inside, leaving Colonel Brand and me on the pavement. I want to make this bit quite clear, if you don't mind. He moved the car out to the middle — there were several others there, all in a row — and then he came back and said, "Do come up, just for a few minutes, it's only a quarter past eleven," and I said: "Don't think me awfully ungracious, but I'm really not in a fit state. Make my apologies to Mrs. What's-her-name, and for pity s sake let me go on sleeping."

So he said, "All right," and went in, and I went across and got into the car. It was a bit public there, so in order not to look too much like an exhibit in a glass case, instead of sitting on the seat I arranged myself in my old position, that is to say, on the floor leaning back against the seat, and I closed my eyes once more.

I don't know how long the particular lacuna lasted, but the next thing I was aware of was that we were no longer standing still. We were proceeding along the road at a rate of knots. This didn't worry me, of course, because it only meant that Colonel Brand had started up without calling me and was running me home, but when we shot across Putney Bridge it was clear that there was something wrong somewhere.

There just aren't any bridges between Queen Anne's Mansions and where I live, so I raised myself up a few inches and took a cautious look forrard. That did give me a surprise if you like, because it wasn't Colonel Brand driving. It was a much smaller man, in a bowler hat.

Well, it didn't take me very long to realise that this cove, whoever he was, had walked in and stolen the car without noticing that he'd got me too, and I wished him joy of me.

The question was how best to deal with the situation without spoiling it. In theory one would have throttled the desperado from behind with one hand and stopped the car with the other. In actual practice it wouldn't have worked. To begin with, we were averaging a good forty and meeting stuff which was doing a jolly sight more, so we should have been safe for a head-on, and to my mind a head-on collision, though the quickest, is not the best method of pulling up. I know because I've tried it. There was another thing, too. Even if we'd had luck and not crashed,

26

and I'd handed my man over to a bobby, he'd have probably got off in the long run by saying he'd only borrowed the car.

So I came to the conclusion that it would be a far better show to sit tight and see where we went. As you probably know, it's the receivers of stolen cars who are the important people to catch.

I huddled down as much out as sight as possible and did my utmost not to doze off, but I'm afraid I must have done, because I found some time later we'd left the main road without my knowledge and were going through a whole lot of narrow country lanes.

Finally, after a good long time, on the way up a big hill, we turned in at some gates and stopped. My friend got down and opened the doors of obviously a garage, turned the car round and backed it in. I decided that the time was still unripe for making my presence known so I let him switch off the lights and lock up undisturbed.

As soon as his footsteps had died away I got out of the car and had a look around. At least it wasn't a look round, it was more of a feel round, it wouldn't have done to show a light. The garage was a fair size, and there was another car in it, so the gang or what-not had evidently had a good day. The doors were firmly padlocked on the outside, but that wasn't very serious because the staples the padlock was fastened to were bolted through the doors, with nuts of those, bolts on the inside. All one had to do was to undo the nuts with a spanner and emerge, which I did.

On my left, as I came out, I could just distinguish the shape of a medium-sized house which clearly belonged to the garage. I tip-toed down to the drive gates to find out what the house was called, but that was N.B.G. (no *blooming* good) because the gates had just been repainted — they were still wet — and for the moment they hadn't got a name on them at all so I walked back into the garden and took enough particulars of the house to be able to know it again.

There was a light in one of the ground-floor windows, but the curtains were drawn and one couldn't see in.

However, I'd found the place and it couldn't run away, so that was all right, but somehow, the more considered things the more bewildered I got.

One would have expected to be taken to some hive of industry in or near London, with rows of men slapping red paint on to green cars, and blue paint on to grey cars, and altering engine-numbers and so on, but this gentleman's charmingly appointed residence, standing in its own well-timbered grounds well, it didn't quite fit into the picture, but then things don't always fit into the picture.

All the same, I didn't see the fun of hanging about all night, and I was determined that Brand should have his car back whatever happened, and it was my only means of getting back to London, so it seemed wisest to make certain of the car first.

I went back to the garage and shoved it out.

Fortunately the little bit of drive sloped down to the gates, and the road outside was down-hill, too, so I was able to get in and run something like three hundred yards without starting the engine or making any noise.

I pulled up by the side of the road and thought some more, and the more I thought, the more I jibbed at the idea of going away without being able to identify the man. It seemed so feeble, and while I don't mind doing anything wrong, within reason, I'm blowed if I'll do anything feeble. There were still lights on downstairs. The man himself opened the door, and the moment I saw him I began to have my first doubt as to whether there mightn't have been a mistake somewhere. He didn't look at all the sort of person you'd expect to steal motor cars. He was between forty-five and fifty, and most friendly. He never asked me what I wanted. He simply said: "Glory be! Can you draw a cork?"

I said: "Can I draw a cork? Of course I can, don't be ridiculous. Why?" Then he told me. He said: "We're in a dreadful predicament. I've made £5000 in the City today. We've only one bottle of whisky worthy of the occasion, and I've got a sprained wrist and I can't trust my wife."

I said: "I'm sorry you can't trust your wife, but have you tried knocking the neck of the bottle off?"

He said: "My dear man, it's ninety years old, come along", and he took me through into a little smoking-room where he introduced me to his wife. She was an extremely charming woman in a *négligée* that made even me blink. It fairly took the cake for negligence. We said: "How do you do."

Next they introduced me to the bottle with the cork which refused to be drawn, but it didn't persist in its refusal very long. When it was safely out we all had some of this gorgeous stuff in liqueur glasses. Do you know, it was impossible to tell it from the finest old brandy. It was like milk — no, better than milk.

We sort of sat and chatted, and they gave me my position which, by the way, was six miles from Guildford, so I must have just nodded a bit on the way down.

Time went on and I was wondering how on earth to introduce the subject of his being a thief without striking too discordant a note, when my eye was caught by an engraving of the Close at Rugby hanging on the wall.

He saw me looking at it, and he said: "Where you there by any chance?" and I said: "Yes." Then he asked me what house I was in, and I told him, and he said: "Whitelaw's? Were you in Whitelaw's? So was I. That means we shall have to have another." (Quite inevitable, of course.)

Actually it meant more than that. It meant I couldn't run him in whatever he'd done. Anyway, he poured out another modicum all round of this priceless liquid and we went on swapping lies about the Bodger and Puff and Bull and various other people who are now either bishops or angels, until I suddenly caught sight of the time, half-past one. I jumped up to go, but first they wouldn't hear of it. Why not stay the night and go up to London in the morning? You've no idea how difficult it was to get away. It was even more difficult to prevent them walking down to the car with me, and that really would have been awkward.

We continued to swear undying friendship until we were too far apart to shout, me feeling no end of a hypocrite, mind you, but when I was safely out of earshot I broke into a brisk trot, because any minute they might have noticed that the garage doors were open.

I found the car all right and started back to London. There was a small village about a mile further on (I don't know where it was because it didn't say on it), and halfway along the main street of this village there was a cottage which was evidently the police station. Just as I was getting to it "the" policeman ran out bang in front of me, and he was the largest and fattest policeman I've ever seen. He was trying to do his belt up as he ran, and it wouldn't meet, and he scuttled along in the glare of my head-lights dodging from side to side just as rabbits sometimes do. I had to pull up to avoid running over him, and it wouldn't have done to do that that because I hadn't my driving licence with me. He asked me if I was going past Bolton's Corner. I hadn't the faintest idea, of course, never having heard of the place, but I offered to drive him there if he'd show me the way. He got in and the car promptly developed a heavy list.

On the way along I asked him: "What's the trouble at Bolton's Corner?" and he explained that some people had broken into a garage and stolen a motor car. The police were out all over the shop blocking the roads and so on to prevent them getting out of the district. One of the places where they were shoving up a barrier was this Bolton's Corner where we were going to.

This looked cheerful. I worked it out that it couldn't be me they were after because there'd hardly been time, but in any case it would mean my being held up for goodness knows how long, and asked a whole lot of silly questions.

Presently we arrived at this place and found an inspector and two constables very industriously rigging up a barricade of scaffold poles. They'd got a small hand-cart, too, and some red lamps, but it didn't look very impressive.

We stopped and got out, and the inspector came up and thanked me very civilly for having given his man a lift.

He clearly recognised I was respectable and all that, but his instructions were to let no one through. I said: "That's all right, Inspector, *of course* you've got to obey orders, and I like your barrier, but are you *quite* sure you've chosen the best place for it?" And I took him back to a little bridge I'd just crossed and said: "There now, that's lovely and narrow; you could hold it against an army."

He quite agreed and they took down their poles and things from in front of me and solemnly carted them back to this bridge behind me, which only goes to show that there are more ways than one of passing a barrier.

I didn't wait to see what sort of a job they made of it because I was beginning to feel sleepy again. In fact, my recollections of driving up to Town are distinctly hazy, but I got there somehow or other.

I even managed to park the car with meticulous care in the exact position it had been taken from in Queen Anne's Mansions courtyard. My first really clear impression was standing on the running-board and comparing my wrist-watch with the clock on the dash. They'd both apparently stopped at half-past eleven. I thought: "That's funny," and I walked across to the ball porter and asked him what the time was and he said, "Half-past eleven."

The Dream

THEY'VE ASKED ME to tell you about another of my experiences, and I think it wouldn't be a bad idea to try and describe to you a dream I often have.

Before describing the dream itself it may be as well to explain a few things about it.

First of all, I've had it some fifteen or twenty times altogether at quite irregular intervals. Sometimes it gives me a miss for two years, at others it will happen twice in six months. There's no knowing.

It began—to visit me—when I was eight or nine years old, and I used to think then that it was just the same dream each time, but it wasn't, and it isn't. The general setting, or *locale*, is the same, but there's a gradual moving forward of events which makes it somewhat interesting — to me, at any rate — and just a bit creepy.

It always begins in exactly the same way. I am walking up a broad flight of stairs in a very large house. The carpet is dark-blue and very thick, so thick that you sink right in.

The walls are all white.

The time, as a rule, is between eleven and twelve at night. It's evidently a party I'm coming to, and I'm rather late for it. My left forefinger is poking a piece of paper down into my waistcoat pocket, and I'm aware in some occult way that it's the ticket for my hat and coat.

The whole place seems deserted except for me, not even anyone to take my name and announce me. In fact, I'm not *rather* late, I'm *very* late.

At the top of the stairs there's a broad sort of landing-place, and, immediately facing me, a very massive mahogany door with a large cut-glass knob. Through this door I go.

In my very young days I used to have quite a job to push it open, but now it's merely heavy and solid.

There's a screen inside the door which cuts me off from the rest of the room, and it just gives me the opportunity to pull down my waistcoat. I walk, with a certain amount of diffidence, round the screen. It's a great big room — very high and brilliantly lighted. The walls are white and the carpet blue — like the stairs — and the furniture is very dark oak.

The scene is rather peculiar. There must be at least forty or fifty men in the room, and they are all sitting on chairs in front of a little platform against the far wall. They aren't sitting in rows, but just anyhow. It looks as though they've drawn up their chairs as near the platform as they can get. I expect that's what happens, really, but I've never got there early enough to see.

They are all much of the same class, as far as general appearance goes; but their ages are widely different. They range from twenty or less right up to seventy and more.

I used to wonder, many years ago, what it was all about, but now I realise that all these people are watching, with very great interest, a conversation which is taking place between a man and a woman. Incidentally, she is the only woman in the room.

These two are sitting on chairs on the dais or platform. It's quite a low platform really — not more than a foot high.

I say they're watching the conversation because I'm sure that unless one happens to be in the very

34

front row it isn't possible to catch more than a word here and there.

The *man* on the platform doesn't call for any particular remark — at least, I don't know — it *is* rather funny about him.

He is evidently just one of the audience who has been invited up, as it were, and I've usually seen him a few times before in the body of the room. But the thing is that once a man has spent the evening on the platform he never appears again.

Now we come to the lady. She is very beautiful — almost too beautiful to be respectable. In fact, if one didn't actually know... However, when I say respectable, I don't mean that she would faint clean away if anyone said damn; but one would hesitate before digging her in the ribs on short acquaintance.

As far as I can tell, she's on the tall side, and very graceful. I've never seen her standing up. She looks as though she could dance well. By dance I mean waltz, of course. She has lovely copper-coloured hair, and she's had the sense not to cut it off. She apparently believes in looking like a woman and not like an ungainly boy. Most unfashionable — but then you must remember that this is a dream.

She's usually dressed in a simple black evening-frock and a hat. The hat is rather of the — I think it's called the turban type. It's a little difficult to describe. It's got a sort of asprey — no, osprey — thing that points backwards and downwards, rather like the tail of the comet does. I think Miss Lily Elsie wore something like that in *The Merry Widow* (if she doesn't mind my dragging her in).

When I say she's wearing a simple black frock, I mean one of those simple little frocks which you can pick up anywhere for fifty or sixty guineas.

And it's never the same dress twice.

While she's sitting down she isn't having a perpetual struggle to make her skirt cover her knees. Not that I've any quarrel with knees — *qua* knees — but those rows of bony excrescences which stick out at you in the Tube, well, surely some of them might be left to the imagination. In fact, if things go on as they are doing now, one won't want an imagination at all, and then what?

To go back to the lady's hat for a moment, I must confess that it rather beats me — why she's wearing one at all, that is — because she must be in her own house.

You can tell that from the way she behaves—I mean, that she's obviously acting as hostess, and her manner is a treat to watch.

She sits quietly in her chair without looking as if she'd been spilt into it, and she doesn't fidget. She hasn't any of those irritating little affectations which one often sees. She doesn't drag out a repair outfit every two minutes and plaster a lot of stuff on her face. Perhaps she doesn't have to. I don't believe she'd even powder her nose in public. Oh, I know that on this subject I'm only a locust crying in the wilderness, but it *is* refreshing to see anyone who isn't ashamed of her complexion.

I've mentioned before that the conversation, or whatever it is, between the good lady and the man on the platform is so quiet that I've never been able to hear her voice, but there's no doubt in my mind that it's the kind that anyone vulgar, who wished to be extra offensive, would describe as a "refained voice"; but he wouldn't be there, so it doesn't matter.

I've racked my brains trying to imagine what on earth they can be talking about for such a long time. In the early part *she* seems to be asking questions and getting very deferential answers. Perhaps she's applying some sort of test. Later on it's more as though she is giving information or instructions, and he just puts in a word here and there.

At about half-past twelve she usually lights a cigarette. Between you and me, I think it's a signal as much as anything to tell all the rest of us that we can smoke if we like. Some of us do.

Now, it's rather a funny thing about the time. More often than not the place where I'm standing gives me a view of a clock there is on the mantelpiece. It's one of those clocks which pretend they haven't got any works, like the women of the present day. You know them — er, the clocks. All you can see is a sheet of plate-glass with the figures and hands on it, and the hands go round in some mysterious way. This clock goes and it's right. *How* do I know it's right? Let's see, how *do* I know it's right? Oh, yes, because it always indicates the time of about one hour after I've gone to sleep, and that may vary quite a lot.

As regards the age of the lady — well, it's a little hard to say. In my extreme youth she was about as old as an aunt. When I grew up she seemed more like a sister, and now I'm blowed if I know how old she is. Early thirties probably. It's rather unusual to grow *past* anyone.

I think I said at the beginning that there aren't quite enough chairs for everyone, and those who come late — like me — have to stand up at the back. All the same, it becomes apparent every now and then during the evening that there is a vacant chair a little way in. It's always a mystery to me *how* this happens, because no one would ever seem to go out (only a blind man would), but when it *does* happen one of the men at the back sort of tiptoes in and takes it.

We just settle amongst ourselves who, like you do in the Tube — "That's all right, I'm getting out at the next station" — you know. A man who has once sat down always has a chair after that, so you see there's a process going on all through the years whereby everyone gradually works forward to the front and eventually finishes up on the platform. It has often, undoubtedly, been my turn to take a vacant chair, but some instinct has always warned me not to. Even our hostess has noticed it, and she's occasionally looked at me as though to say: "Aren't you going to sit down?" but I've always half-shaken my head and let someone else have it — the chair, that is. Then she has given a slight, very slight, shrug of the shoulders, and I've felt rather ungracious and left it at that. I know now why I don't sit down, and I'll tell you about that presently.

It's extremely difficult to give you the facts about this dream in their proper order, because there isn't a proper order, and it differs in so many ways from ordinary dreams. There are none of the mad things in it that you ordinarily get... The one I'm telling you about is so abnormally normal.

The one constantly variable factor is the man on the platform, and it's rotten bad luck that I've always been too late to see how he comes to be chosen out of all the others. He was once just sitting down, but that's the nearest I've ever got.

It used to strike me what a rag it would be if only I could recognise anyone there. After all, it stands to reason that all these other people must be dreaming, too — and then we could compare notes next day.

Well, one night the man on the platform was a man, a rather famous man, whom I knew very well. When I say I knew him very well, I really mean that I knew his secretary very well, which is infinitely better, believe me. So next morning I rang her up — the secretary — and said, "I say, I wish you'd fix me up an appointment with the old man some time during the day, because I want to see him very particularly." And she said, "I'm afraid you can't because he was found dead in bed this morning."

Wasn't it just my luck? Fearful hard lines on him, too, of course, but it absolutely dished my chance of finding out what the dream meant.

However, the Fates were kind. Three or four years later I again saw a man on the platform whom I knew perfectly well. His name was Ribblechick, but he couldn't help that, poor chap. He recognized me, too, and we grinned at each other, and I thought now it's all right — he'll have heard her speak, and will be able to tell me what she is — if not who.

So next morning I trotted round—they lived quite near us—and will you believe it, the whole house was upside down. He, poor old Ribblechick, had been found dead in bed, too. Heart-failure, they said it was.

Please don't think that I'm suggesting for a moment that it was anything but the purest coincidence that these two unfortunate people happened to die in the same way. But all the same, each time I dream my dream nowadays, and a chair does fall vacant, I still let someone else have it, and the good lady still shrugs her shoulders.

Wottie

THE PREPARATORY school I went to was near Haywards Heath, about sixteen miles from Brighton—in Sussex, you know. The headmaster was a man called Mercer, and he knew his job.

He taught us cricket and rugger, and how to behave, and (I believe) one or two other things.

There was nothing at all petty about him. He didn't make us walk two and two on Sunday afternoons, but he discouraged us from *openly* laughing at schools who did. If anyone attempted to put on "side" he promptly thrashed him. Altogether old Mercer was a sportsman, and so, incidentally, was Mrs Mercer.

As regards tuck-shops, we were pretty well off. There were two. For instance, Russian toffee was eight a penny instead of ten, as it was at Jackson's, and you didn't get quite such a big ice for threepence, but it was clearer.

Also there was Ma Wottlespoon. That's what she was known as, but I ought to point out that it was quite a courtesy and proleptic use of the title "Ma." The lady was, to the best of my belief, a complete and utter spinster. She was fair and plump, but not by any means old. She was very dignified, too. For instance, as soon as you got your "eleven" or your "fifteen" you could call her "Wottie", but not before. She was awfully decent about tick, and had rather prominent front teeth.

That's the sort of person she was. We all liked her, of course, ever so, but Ackroyd major went a bit too far in my opinion, and got quite sloppy about her and it was rather distressing, because he was a particular friend of mine.

Not only that, we were both of us getting fairly senior, and old Mercer expected us to set an example to the rest of the school, so you see how difficult it was when he — Ackroyd, that is — went and developed this passion for Wottie. I was terrified that other people might notice it.

He used to give her presents. There was a perfectly appalling inkstand, I remember, and I had to present it because he was too shy. I was shy too, of course, but not as shy as he was. I shall never forget it. We had to wait till the shop was empty, then I went in and thrust the inkstand at her. Ackroyd hung about outside. She was perfectly charming, as always, though I'm quite sure she must have wondered what it all meant. At least, I don't know. They say women understand these things. She tried to give me a sausage-roll, and it was dreadfully awkward. I went outside and kicked Ackroyd, and that was my first experience as a liaison officer.

At all events, this was the pitch things had got to just before the middle of a certain summer term. Then there came a day of tragedy. It wasn't all tragic by any manner of means. In fact, as days go, it began jolly well.

There was a whacking great thunderstorm at about six o'clock in the morning, and the whole basement of the house was flooded to a depth of nearly two feet. It was owing to some grating getting stopped up. Old Mercer allowed us to bale it out in our pyjamas instead of doing early school, and you could actually swim in the coal-cellar. On the top of all this it was the morning we had hot rolls for breakfast and a half-holiday, so what more could you want?

However, after dinner someone strolled down to Wottie's for an ice, and came racing back with the news that she'd disappeared. She'd got up and dressed during the night and not come back.

We naturally tore down to the shop, about twenty of us, to verify this, and found her mother in a great state of mind. In another walk of life she'd leave been sitting with her apron over her head — if you know what I mean. She was sure that something terrible must have happened to her daughter.

We weren't old enough to do anything but agree, so we bought a few things out of sympathy and faded away. During the next few days, sundry rumours filtered into the school, via boot-boys and people, of woods being searched and ponds dragged, but without success.

Wottie never came back, and it came to be generally accepted that she had made away with herself owing to a fruitless love-affair.

Ackroyd was nearly prostrate with grief. With any encouragement at all he'd have persuaded himself that it was entirely on his account that she'd gone out and committed this suicide. What did I think? I said I thought not, unless she'd been driven to it by the inkstand. Whereupon we had words, in the course of which we forgot Wottie - for the time being.

I'm afraid you will have to excuse this story for being rather disjointed, but it's rather a disjointed story. Nothing more happened for about three weeks, and then something did.

You should know that Mrs. Mercer, our headmaster's wife, was an extremely nice woman, and, like so many extremely nice women, she had an awful lot of brothers — about eight — and one or two of these brothers used to come down to the school for most week-ends.

It's a matter of considerable surprise to me that they ever came a second time in view of what they had to put up with. Reels of cotton unwound themselves in tin boxes on the tops of their wardrobes. Alarm-clocks went off under their beds at 3 a.m., and those who slept with their mouths open were fed with pellets of soap. In fact, they were made thoroughly welcome.

Well, the one who was coming this particular Saturday was Julian. We didn't call him that, but that's who he was. He was immensely tall and bowled leg-breaks.

Now, it so happened that the rest of the school were being taken into Brighton to see the last day of Sussex *v.* Middlesex. Ackroyd and I weren't going, because the following Saturday old Mercer was going to take us to a place near Sheffield Park to see the South Africans play someone or other. So this left Ackroyd and me entirely on our own, and we thought it would be rather a good tweak to go down to the station and meet old Julian and carry his bag up. He would, or should, think how kind of its it was, and while he was still in this frame of mind we should stop for a breather just outside the tuck-shop and — er — *voila!*

We knew everyone's habits, and as Julian had always come by the two-fifteen we duly met it, but to our extreme chagrin it arrived without him, and so did the next train, so we gave it up. We decided that it was a beastly swizzle, all our plans being upset like this, and we promptly cast about in our minds for some mischief to get into.

Ackroyd "voted" that we went and tried to hire the tandem from Hilton's (Hilton's was the local bicycle hop where we got our hair cut) and then rode to Blane's Hill Quarry. I said: "Good egg." I said it with special care-freedom because I hadn't any money at all, whereas I knew he'd got five bob. He was the pampered son of an only father and mother, and they'd sent it him that very morning. So, as I say, I concurred with this proposal.

There was a strong element of doubt about our getting this tandem because the man hadn't ever let us have it. He said we weren't old enough. However, we were lucky. He wasn't there — it was only Mrs Bicycle, and she raised no objections. Ackroyd planked down his half-crown just as though it were a penny, and away we went.

We didn't attempt to mount the machine outside the shop, because we didn't know how, and the saddles were too high, anyway, so we wheeled it up to Wottie's. We leant it against the window and went inside to see how far Ackroyd's remaining half-crown could be made to go.

We got a reasonably large pork-pie, which was our fashionable "stodge" just then, but we couldn't get any éclairs to go with it owing to Wottie herself being dead and so on, so we had to be content with half a chocolate cake for second course, and four bottles of stone ginger-beer.

We tied these stores about the wretched tandem until it looked like a Christmas-tree, and wheeled it clear of the village.

We then proceeded to learn to ride it. Ackroyd bagged the front seat, so I held the machine upright while he got on, and when he was on I pushed it a few yards and got on too — in perfectly good faith, but Ackroyd promptly steered us into the right-hand ditch.

There wasn't any water in it, but it was none the less a ditch.

Well, we picked ourselves up and brushed each other down and got on again. After all, you can't expect to be able to ride a tandem first go off, but when we continued to crash time after time into the right-hand hedge without the slightest sign of improvement, I began to feel it in my bones that we weren't, somehow, getting the best out of our machine.

I raised the matter with Ackroyd the next time we fell off. I said: "I say, Ackroyd, you might let me sit in front. You can't steer for nuts."

He demurred on the grounds that it was his half-crown which had paid for the hire of the blooming thing, and he could steer it if be liked.

I said he obviously couldn't, and that he'd better let me have a go while the front wheel was anything like round. I also agreed to pay him one and three-pence, which I ear-marked out of my return journey money at the end of term. That did it, and we swapped over.

Just as we were going to remount I noticed that the string of the pork-pie parcel had somehow got looped over the front lamp-bracket, and it was preventing the handle-bar from being turned to the left at all. I just unlooped it. It was no good telling Ackroyd, because he'd only have wanted to try sitting in front again.

As it was, we began to make progress. I don't wish to spot myself in the very least, but we did get along quite well, especially on the straight, and there was only a slight falling off at one or two of the sharper corners.

Well, we got to Blane's Hill Quarry all right — it was only about four miles — and sat down on the edge to enjoy ourselves.

I should perhaps mention that this quarry was hopelessly out of bounds, because it was extremely dangerous, which made it all the more attractive, and it was a lovely day, but the food was not all it might have been. Anything but. I don't know what the shelf-life of a pork-pie is, but when we come to break this one open we found a sort of grey feathery deposit on the top of the pork. If it had been an accumulator I should have said it was sulphating.

It tasted so mouldy that we could hardly finish it, and the shortcomings of the chocolate cake made us still further deplore the death or what not of Wottie. However, at the noontide of youth (we were both twelve) moods soon pass, and we looked round for some convenient method of disposing of the empty ginger-beer bottles. We didn't want to leave them lying about.

Now, there was a small stone hut with a slate roof down at the bottom of the quarry, about fifty feet below us, which really might have been put there on purpose.

We registered two direct hits on it, but the roof proved obstinate and the bottles merely bounced off. Not to be borne for a moment. Ackroyd found a piece of flint the size of a football and said: "I dare you to throw that down."

Mind you, I'm not defending my action for a moment — it was dastardly — but you know what it is when you are dared to do anything. I simply *had* to pitch this young boulder over, and it went "plunk" straight through the roof and left a great gaping hole in the slates.

There was no chance of hurting anyone because it was only a sort of store-shed. We found out afterwards that they kept the dynamite and detonators there for blasting in the quarry, but we oughtn't to have dropped rocks on it just the same.

The next thing Ackroyd did was to fall over the edge. It was a judgment on him, because he was reaching for something still larger to throw, and he made a slight miscalculage and lost his balance. I thought he'd gone right to the bottom, and I was a bit worried, but actually there was a ledge sticking out a few feet down, and on this ledge he — lodged. It was covered with brambles, and he got so involved that I had to climb down and undo him.

While we were messing about down there we both began to notice a most peculiar — what shall I say? - lack of freshness in the air. Most marked it was, and it seemed to be coming from the mouth of a small tunnel driven into the face of the stone just behind us.

I said: "Something's died", and Ackroyd said: "Let's go in and see what it is." I wasn't frightfully keen personally, but he would go, so I had to follow. We had to duck our heads to get in, and there wasn't room to walk two abreast. It was pretty dark, too, after the glare outside, and the atmosphere — well, it was indescribable.

We'd only gone three or four yards when Ackroyd stooped over something lying on the ground; then he suddenly gave a most fearful yell and said: "By gosh, it's Wottie — let me out", and he turned round and tried to charge past me, but the place was so beastly narrow that we almost got jammed, and while we were fighting to get free I caught a glimpse, over his shoulder, of a ghastly object with an almost black face grinning at us. It wouldn't have been recognisable at all if it hadn't been for the rather prominent front teeth. One look was enough for me — I bolted for the entrance for all I was worth, with Ackroyd after me — still yelling.

It may sound cowardly now, but we'd neither of us seen anyone dead before, and what with one thing and another it came as a bit of a shock. I've no recollection at all of getting back to the tandem, but I do know we rode it across a cornfield without falling off, which only shows what absolute panic will do.

We'd recovered somewhat by the time we got back to the school and we went and had a long jaw behind the pav. about what was to be done.

If we'd been a little older we should have gone straight to old Mercer and owned up, but we were so afraid of what might happen to us for going to the quarry at all, let alone bashing in that roof, that we decided to trust to luck and keep quiet, and, strange to say, we were never found out.

* * *

After thirty odd years I was almost beginning to regard the incident as closed until, about a couple of months ago, I got a letter from a cousin of mine.

He lives down in Sussex, and he said, in his letter, that they'd just laid out a new golf course near his place. Would we go down for the opening and watch him miss his first tee shot? He'd been elected president of the club, or something, and had to drive off before a cheering multitude.

Well, my wife and I went down on the great day and saw him carry the first hazard of the course in brilliant fashion.

This hazard turned out to be a corner of my dear old friend, Blane's Hill Quarry. It had been disused for some years, so they told me, but there it still was, as large as life. That's the great thing about a quarry

- when it's done with it's got to stop. You can't pull it down or turn it into flats.

I even recognised the ruins of the old dynamite store. The historic tunnel where Ackroyd and I had found — what we had found, was right away on the far side, and there wasn't a chance of going to look for it just then. But after dinner that night (my cousin had a lot of people there) I told them the whole story — all about Wottie and the tandem, and finding the body, and so on - just as I've told it to you, only *they* didn't believe it. They said I'd made it all up — as though one would. They were so jolly certain about it not being true that they laid me ten to one in gin and bitters that I couldn't take them to the place and show them the tunnel.

I said: "Done with you", and it was finally arranged for us all to meet at the Golf Club next morning, and then I was to lead them to the tragic spot. They called it the gruesome grotto.

By the by, one man dining there was the coroner for the district, and he pointed out that if we found so much as a single bone he'd have to hold an inquest. They do, you know. Why, they once found a mummy in the cloakroom at King's Cross, and they solemnly sat on the good lady to find out what she'd died of about seven thousand years before.

At any rate, we all met next morning and walked round the edge of the quarry till we got to the point just above the ruins of the store-shed. The ledge was still there, and I slithered down on to it. The others were still so certain that it was all a leg-pull that they wouldn't come down with me. They all stood at the top and jeered. The whole place was a mass of brambles and weeds, but I found the tunnel all right. That fetched 'em. They all came tumbling down and fairly fought to get the entrance clear.

As soon as it was possible my cousin and I squeezed in, and we found an absolutely perfect skeleton — of a sheep.

Well, of course, they reckoned I'd won all right, and that it was very handsome of me to have thrown in a skeleton as well when it wasn't in the contract, even if it wasn't the right kind of skeleton. But up at the club-house afterwards, over my winnings, one of them said: "It's all very well, you know, but quite apart from your being a couple of heartless young devils, I can't think why you didn't go back next day out of sheer curiosity, and then you'd have found that it *was* only a sheep."

And I said : "Yes, we did."

My Adventure in Norfolk

I DON'T KNOW how it is with you, but during February ary *my* wife generally says to me: "Have you thought at all about what we are going to do for August?" And, of course, I say, "No," and then she begins looking through the advertisements of bungalows to let.

Well, this happened last year, as usual, and she eventually produced one that looked possible. It said: "Norfolk—Hickling Broad—Furnished Bungalow— Garden—Garage, Boathouse," and all the rest of it—Oh—*and* plate and linen. It also mentioned an exorbitant rent. I pointed out the bit about the rent, but my wife said: "Yes, you'll have to go down and see the landlord, and get him to come down. They always do." As a matter of fact, they always don't, but that's a detail.

Anyway, I wrote off to the landlord and asked if he could arrange for me to stay the night in the place to see what it was really like. He wrote back and said: "Certainly," and that he was engaging Mrs. So-and-So to come in and "oblige me," and make up the beds and so forth.

I tell you, we do things thoroughly in our family—I have to sleep in all the beds, and when I come home my wife counts the bruises and decides whether they will do or not.

At any rate, I arrived, in a blinding snowstorm, at about *the* most desolate spot on God's earth. I'd come to Potter Heigham by train, and been driven on (it was a good five miles from the station). Fortunately, Mrs. Selston, the old lady who was going to "do" for me, was there, and she'd lighted a fire, and cooked me a steak, for which I was truly thankful.

I somehow think the cow, or whatever they get steaks off, had only died that morning. It was very-er—obstinate. While I dined, she talked to me. She *would* tell me all about an operation her husband had just had. *All* about it. It was almost a lecture on surgery. The steak was rather underdone, and it sort of made me feel I was illustrating her lecture. Anyway she put me clean off my dinner, and then departed for the night.

I explored the bungalow and just had a look outside. It was, of course, very dark, but not snowing quite so hard. The garage stood about fifteen yards from the back door. I walked round it, but didn't go in. I also went down to the edge of the broad, and verified the boathouse. The whole place looked as though it might be all right in the summertime, but just then it made one wonder why people ever wanted to go to the North Pole.

Anyhow, I went indoors, and settled down by the fire. You've no idea how quiet it was; even the water-fowl had taken a night off—at least, they weren't working.

At a few minutes to eleven I heard the first noise there'd been since Mrs. What's-her-name—Selston-had cleared out. It was the sound of a car. If it had gone straight by I probably shouldn't have noticed it at all, only it didn't go straight by; it seemed to stop farther up the road, before it got to the house. Even that didn't make much impression. After all, cars *do* stop.

It must have been five or ten minutes before it was borne in on me that it hadn't gone on again. So I got up and looked out of the window. It had left off snowing, and there was a glare through the gate that showed that there were headlamps somewhere just out of sight. I thought I might as well stroll out and investigate.

I found a fair-sized limousine pulled up in the middle of the road about twenty yards short of my gate. The light was rather blinding, but when I got close to it I found a girl with the bonnet open, tinkering with the engine. Quite an attractive young female, from what one could see, but she was so muffled up in furs that it was rather hard to tell.

I said: "Er—good evening—anything I can do."

She said she didn't know what was the matter. The engine had just stopped, and wouldn't start again. And it *had!* It wouldn't even turn, either with the self-starter or the handle. The whole thing was awfully hot, and I asked her whether there was any water in the radiator. She didn't see why there shouldn't be, there always had been. This didn't strike me as entirely conclusive. I said, we'd better put some in, and see what happened. She said, why not use snow? But I thought not. There was an idea at the back of my mind that there was some reason why it was unwise to use melted snow, and it wasn't until I arrived back with a bucketful that I remembered what it was. Of course—goitre.

When I got back to her she'd got the radiator cap off, and inserted what a Danish friend of mine calls a "funeral". We poured a little water in... Luckily I'd warned her to stand clear. The first tablespoonful that went in came straight out again, red hot, and blew the "funeral" sky-high. We waited a few minutes until things had cooled down a bit, but it was no go. As fast as we poured water in it simply ran out again into the road underneath. It was quite evident that she'd been driving with the radiator bone dry, and that her engine had seized right up.

I told her so. She said:

"Does that mean I've got to stop here all night?"

I explained that it wasn't as bad as all that; that is, if she cared to accept the hospitality of my poor roof (and it *was* a poor roof—it let the wet in). But she wouldn't hear of it. By the by, she didn't know the– er—circumstances, so it wasn't that. No, she wanted to leave the car where it was and go on on foot.

I said:

"Don't be silly, it's miles to anywhere."

However, at that moment we heard a car coming along the road, the same way as she'd come. We could see its lights, too, although it was a very long way off. You know how flat Norfolk is—you can see a terrific distance.

I said:

"There's the way out of all your troubles. This thing, whatever it is, will give you a tow to the nearest garage, or at any rate a lift to some hotel."

One would have expected her to show some relief, but she didn't. I began to wonder what she jolly well *did* want. She wouldn't let me help her to stop where she was, and she didn't seem anxious for anyone to help her to go anywhere else.

She was quite peculiar about it. She gripped hold of my arm, and said:

"What do you think this is that's coming?"

I said:

"I'm sure I don't know, being a stranger in these parts, but it sounds like a lorry full of milk cans."

I offered to lay her sixpence about it (this was before the betting-tax came in). She'd have had to pay, too, because it *was* a lorry full of milk cans. The driver had to pull up because there wasn't room to get by.

He got down and asked if there was anything he could do to help. We explained the situation. He said he was going to Norwich, and was quite ready to give her a tow if she wanted it. However, she wouldn't do that, and it was finally decided to shove her car into my garage for the night, to be sent for next day, and the lorry was to take her along to Norwich.

Well, I managed to find the key of the garage, and the lorry-driver—Williams, his name was—and I ran the car in and locked the door. This having been done—(ablative absolute)—I suggested that it was a very cold night. Williams agreed, and said he didn't mind if he did. So I took them both indoors and mixed them a stiff whisky and water each. There wasn't any soda. And, naturally, the whole thing had left *me* very cold, too. I hadn't an overcoat on.

Up to now I hadn't seriously considered the young woman. For one thing it had been dark, *and* there had been a seized engine to look at. Er—I'm afraid that's not a very gallant remark. What I mean is that to anyone with a mechanical mind a motor-car in that condition is much more interesting than—er— well, it *is* very interesting—but why labour the point? However, in the sitting-room, in the lamplight, it was possible to get more of an idea. She was a little older than I'd thought, and her eyes were too close together.

Of course, she wasn't a—how shall I put it? Her manners weren't quite easy and she was careful with her English. *You* know. But that wasn't it. She treated us with a lack of friendliness which was—well, we'd done nothing to deserve it. There was a sort of vague hostility and suspicion, which seemed rather hard lines, considering. Also, she was so anxious to keep in the shadow that if I hadn't moved the lamp away she'd never have got near the fire at all.

And the way she hurried the wretched William over his drink was quite distressing; and foolish, to as *he* was going to drive, but that was her—funne When he'd gone out to start up his engine I asked he if she was all right for money, and she apparently wa Then they started off, and I shut up the place an went upstairs.

There happened to be a local guide-book in m bedroom, with maps in it. I looked at these an couldn't help wondering where the girl in the car ha come from; I mean my road seemed so very unimpo tant. The sort of road one might use if one wanted t avoid people. If one were driving a stolen car, fo instance. This was quite a thrilling idea. I thought i might be worth while having another look at the ca So I once more unhooked the key from the kitchei dresser and sallied forth into the snow. It was a black as pitch, and so still that my candle hardl flickered. It wasn't a large garage, and the car nearl filled it. By the by, we'd backed it in so as to make easier to tow it out again.

The engine I'd already seen, so I squeezed pas along the wall and opened the door in the body par of the car. At least, I only turned the handle, and th door was pushed open from the inside and something—fell out on me. It pushed me quite har and wedged me against the wall. It also knocked th candle out of my hand and left me in the dark—which was a bit of a nuisance. I wondered what on earth th thing was—barging into me like that—so I felt i rather gingerly, and found it was a man—a dea man—with a moustache. He'd evidently been sittin propped up against the door. I managed to put hin back, as decorously as possible, and shut the doo again.

After a lot of grovelling about under the car I found the candle and lighted it, and opened the opposite door and switched on the little lamp in the roof—and then—oo-er!

Of course, I had to make some sort of examination. He was an extremely tall and thin individual. He must have been well over six feet three. He was dark and very cadaverous-looking. In fact, I don't suppose he'd ever looked so cadaverous in his life. He was wearing a trench coat.

It wasn't difficult to tell what he'd died of. He'd been shot through the back. I found the hole just under the right scrofula, or scalpel—what is shoulder-blade, anyway? Oh, clavicle—stupid of me—well, that's where it was, and the bullet had evidently gone through into the lung. I say "evidently," and leave it at that.

There were no papers in his pockets, and no tailor's name on his clothes, but there was a note-case, with nine pounds in it. Altogether a most unpleasant business. Of course, it doesn't do to question the workings of Providence, but one couldn't help wishing it hadn't happened. It was just a little mysterious, too—er—who had killed him. It wasn't likely that the girl had or she wouldn't have been joy-riding about the country with him; and if someone else had murdered him why hadn't she mentioned it? Anyway, she hadn't and she'd gone, so one couldn't do anything for the time being. No telephone, of course. I just locked up the garage and went to bed. That was two o'clock.

Next morning I woke early, for some reason or other, and it occurred to me as a good idea to go and have a look at things—by daylight, and before Mrs. Selston turned up. So I did. The first thing that struck me was that it had snowed heavily during the night, because there were no wheel tracks or foot-prints, and the second was that I'd left the key in the garage door. I opened it and went in. The place was completely empty. No car, no body, no nothing. There was a patch of grease on the floor where I'd dropped the candle, otherwise there was nothing to show I'd been there before. One of two things must have happened: either some people had come along during the night and taken the car away, or else I'd fallen asleep in front of the fire and dreamt the whole thing

Then I remembered the whisky glasses.

They should still be in the sitting-room. I went back to look, and they were, all three of them. So it *hadn't* been a dream and the car *had* been fetched away, but they must have been jolly quiet over it.

The girl had left her glass on the mantel-piece, and it showed several very clearly defined finger-marks Some were mine, naturally, because I'd fetched the glass from the kitchen and poured out the drink for her, but hers, her finger-marks, were clean, and mine were oily, so it was quite easy to tell them apart. It isn't necessary to point out that this glass was very important. There'd evidently been a murder, or some-thing of that kind, and the girl must have known all about it, even if she hadn't actually done it herself, so anything she had left in the way of evidence ought to be handed over to the police; and this was all she *had* left. So I packed it up with meticulous care in an old biscuit-box out of the larder.

When Mrs. Selston came I settled up with her and came back to Town. Oh, I called on the landlord on the way and told him I'd "let him know" about the bungalow. Then I caught my train, and in due course drove straight to Scotland Yard. I went up and saw my friend there. I produced the glass and asked him if his people could identify the marks. He said:

"Probably not," but he sent it down to the fingerprint department and asked me where it came from. I said: "Never you mind; let's have the identification first." He said: "All right."

They're awfully quick, these people—the clerk was back in three minutes with a file of papers. They knew the girl all right. They told me her name and showed me her photograph; not flattering. Quite an adventurous lady, from all accounts. In the early part of her career she'd done time twice for shop-lifting, chiefly in the book department. Then she'd what they call "taken up with" a member of one of those race-gangs one sometimes hears about.

My pal went on to say that there'd been a fight between two of these gangs, in the course of which her friend had got shot. She'd managed to get him away in a car, but it had broken down somewhere in Norfolk. So she'd left it and the dead man in some-one's garage, and had started off for Norwich in a lorry. Only she never got there. On the way the lorry had skidded, and both she and the driver—a fellow called Williams—had been thrown out, and they'd rammed their heads against a brick wall, which everyone knows is a fatal thing to do. At least, it was in their case.

I said: "Look here, it's all very well, but you simply can't know all this; there hasn't been time—it only happened last night."

He said: "Last night be blowed! It all happened in February 1919. The people you've described have been dead for years."

I said: "Oh!"

And to think that I might have stuck to that nine pounds!

A Foggy Evening

I WANT TO make it quite clear from the very beginning that what I am going to tell you now isn't a story in any sense of the word; and it most certainly hasn't got a plot.

If the various happenings I have told you about from time to time had always conveniently arranged themselves into magazine story form, my reputation for telling the truth wouldn't have lasted very long.

As it *is*—or, rather, *as* it is—that reputation is very precious to me, as you can quite imagine.

No, this is just a rambling account of a foggy evening; but it may interest one or two of you as an example of the sort of things that may happen to one, if one'll only let 'em, as it were.

Do you remember the ninth of December last?

Probably not, as such; but if you don't remember the date, you won't have forgotten the fog.

Well, that's when it was, anyway.

It's a little difficult to know where to begin —but there's always the beginning. One might try that.

It must have been about a quarter to seven when I got home, and my wife met me and said:

"You're dining out, *you* are!"

And I said:

"Oh, I am, am I, and what about you, and where am I dining?"

And she said:

"You're dining with the Lees—she's just telephoned to say they're a man short at the last minute, so I've sent them you, and I shall have something on a

63

tray"—which, of course, as you all know, mean nothing on a tray. But that's a detail.

Well, my dear wife and Mrs. Lee seemed to hav disposed of me all right for the evening, so I went u and changed, and in due course arrived at the Lees just before eight, that was. They live about seve minutes' walk from Hampstead Tube Station.

At this time it was beginning to get distinctly fogg I rang the bell and waited, and nothing happened, s I rang again. This time a terrified-looking parlou maid opened the door—with her face like a sheet. S much so, that I asked her what was the matter.

It appeared that there'd been a tragedy just a fe minutes before. The Lees' small son, aged eight, ha been put to bed early, because of the party. He' evidently felt bored and had got out of his room an started sliding down the banisters. Unfortunatel he'd crashed and pitched on to his head on the ha floor.

While the maid was telling me about it, Lee cam to the door himself and fetched me in.

The boy hadn't been moved, and a doctor wa overhauling him. So far, he'd found a very nasty cu on the head, and bad concussion.

Altogether, it was pretty serious.

Mrs. Lee was, naturally, frightfully upset, and an idea of a dinner-party was a clean washout—I mea it was quite out of the question.

So, after some discussion, it was arranged that should stand outside the front door (to avoid its bein constantly opened) and boom the guests off as the arrived. I did this, and explained matters to fiv hungry souls, and they were all very concerned, an quite understood, and they just faded away into th fog again

Doctors kept dashing up, too. I let *them* in. The Lees must have put out a regular district call for doctors. You know what it is when there's an accident. You telephone wildly round to all the doctors you can think of—and, of course, they're all out—and you leave a message and then they all roll up in a bunch.

Most of these came out again, and one of them told me that Master Billy had come round—no bones broken—cut being stitched up—in fact, outlook rather brighter. I did Cerberus on the top step for a few minutes more, until all was quiet, and then I cleared off, too.

The fog had been getting steadily worse every minute, and it was now a real, proper pea-souper.

I started off down the hill to where I thought I'd left Hampstead Tube Station, but it didn't seem to be there. However, that didn't worry me overmuch because, well, I don't suppose many people will agree with me, but if you rule out danger to shipping, and flying, and trains, and things like that, fogs can be rather jolly.

I mean, when you can hardly see the ground, and you think you've crossed the road and haven't, and are really back on the same side again—and all that.

Then again, you've always got the chance of something amusing happening any minute.

Well, to go back to the evening we are talking about. I was still casting about for Hampstead Tube Station, and not finding it, but I did find a taxi; I ran into it. It was right across the pavement with its nose sticking into the railings. There didn't seem to be any sign of a driver. He may have got tired of being a taxi-driver and just gone home (people do!).

I opened the door and looked inside—and two voices said: "Go away!" *They* were evidently fog lovers, too. So I said: "Sorry," and shut the door again, and went on my way down the hill rejoicing—and possibly even humming a sprightly air. That's the best of a fog—you can do all sorts of things you wouldn't do any other time. It's like having a railway carriage to yourself.

Well, by this time, it was nearly nine o'clock, and I was getting most infernally hungry. So I gave up looking for the Hampstead Tube, and hunted for a place to get something to eat instead—no matter what it was like—coffee stall—somewhere with steam on the window—fish and chip shop—anything you like. But my luck must have been properly in that evening, because I barged into a bay-tree growing in a tub. There were two of them—standing outside a doorway. Over the door was a red lamp, and it said on it: "The Planet Restaurant".

What do you think of that? A place with bay-trees when I should have fairly leapt at "Sausage and mash, eightpence".

I pushed the door open—swing door it was—and found myself at the bottom of a flight of stairs. The place apparently hadn't got a ground floor at all—probably the upper part over a shop. Red carpet, brass stair rods, white paint, all new and very swagger. I went up the stairs which finished up in a long, narrow room with tables down each side. There were a few people there finishing dinner, but not very many. The place looked as though it hadn't been open very long.

A graceful damsel in a red overall took my hat and coat, and shoved me down at a table. She was sorry it was too late for the dinner, but gave me to understand that the grill was still going strong.

"What about a nice fillet steak?"

I said, "Rather!"—and then she produced a wine list.

Most astounding place! The chef knew his job. The burgundy wasn't half bad, and was properly warmed. In fact, I tell you, that place was living up to its bay-trees for all it was worth.

Well, while I was having dinner, the rest of the people trickled out by ones and twos, until there was only one other man left—besides me.

He was by himself, at the next table but one. I hadn't noticed him before, because there had been other people between. Rum-looking bloke he was. He looked rather like a shortsighted sheep-dog. He wore glasses, which kept on slipping down his nose. They evidently got misty, too, as he was always having to polish them.

He seemed to suffer from chronic hotness and botherdom, and he'd evidently got the idea into his head that he knew me. He kept on looking my way and giving little nods. And I was equally certain that I'd never set eyes on him in my life before. Now here was a slight chance of indulging in a little game which always appeals to me very much.

You play it like this. A man—you don't know from Adam—comes up and wrings you by the hand, and says: "Hallo, old man, how are you?"(It does happen sometimes.) Well, instead of saying: "I'm sorry, sir, but I think you must be making a mistake," you don't. You say: "By Jove, this is nice! What brings you here?" or something original and brilliant like that. And he tells you, and then you lead him on to talk. It's not a bad plan to find out fairly early in the proceedings when and where you last met. Then he may easily ask after some mutual acquaintance and say: "How's So-and-So?" And you say: "Haven't you heard? She's doing very well. She's a missionary in China." And he

says: "Good gracious! Has she chucked the stage?"–
and so on.

You've no idea what fun it is until you've tried it. I
once kept the game going for a whole evening with a
man at the club, and at the end I owned up quite
frankly and said: "Look here, I hope you won't be
frightfully sick, but I've been playing spoof all the
time, and I'm not the bloke you've been taking me for."
And he said: "That's all right, old man, neither am I.
I've been playing spoof, too!" It was really great.

Well, here was the old boy at the next table but one
sort of half-nodding, and fairly asking for it, so I
nodded back as though I'd only just recognized him.
He immediately came along and said: "You've had
your hair cut." And I said: "Quite right, my dear
Watson, I *have* had my hair cut---yesterday, at the
R.A.C., if you want to know." And he said: -Well, do
you know it's altered you so much that I wasn't sure
it was you until you mentioned my name." Just think
of it, his name actually was Watson. I'd only been
quoting Sherlock Holmes in fun. (You know how one
does.)

Of course, this was an absolute gift. No—but
really, wouldn't it have been tempting Providence to
let such a chance slip? I'm sure you've all noticed
that the most amusing and exciting things always
happen to someone else. Ergo, if you can only get
taken for someone else, there's a much better chance
of something amusing and exciting happening to you.
Quite sound reasoning.

Very well, then. He was taking me for someone
else, all right. Let the thing go on.

He said: "This is splendid, we can go on to the
Eldersteins together." And I said: "All for it," wonder-
ing who the El—er—who the Eldersteins might be.
Good old English name, of course. "Was there time

or another glass of port?" He thought there just was, and this gave me time to find out that the Eldersteins gave these mysterious parties every now and then; that I sometimes went, and that to-night was a special night.

He was evidently bursting to tell me why—why it was a special night (and I wanted to know, too, of course). So I said: "Tell me exactly what you've heard." (Rather neat, don't you think?) And he said: "Well, the president really *is* going to be with us," and I tried to look as though I was trying not to look surprised, and wished he'd say what president and where he was president of. But he didn't. All he said was, what fun there'd be about my having had my hair cut; and he chuckled away—quite a nice friendly beast; but I was getting rather bored with having my hair chucked in my teeth.

Presently we paid our bills and started off for the Eldersteins—me taking great care not to let on that I hadn't the vaguest idea where we were going to. Luckily it wasn't far, and the fog was as thick as ever. So we blundered along, round all sorts of corners, barking our shins—and finally we fetched up at a door in some mews. Well, "My dear Watson" gave four taps at this door and a man in chauffeur's uniform opened it.

We went in and found ourselves in a garage. There was a door at the back with a long passage leading on from it. Watson evidently knew the ropes and led the way down this passage.

By this time I really was beginning to hope that he was taking me somewhere not quite respectable. No, but it did rather look like it, didn't it?—going in the back way—four taps on the door—and all that.

However, presently we got to a sort of lobby place, where a maid took our hats and coats and gave us tickets for them. There were evidently a good few people there, judging from the number of coats.

A little way past the lobby was a glass door, and through it we could see into a very large room. There was clearly some sort of entertainment going on several rows of gilt chairs, with people in 'em.

We slipped in quietly and stood by the wall—and the moment we were inside I realized that a woman was doing a recitation, so I tried to get out again, but my dear Watson rather had me by the arm, and one couldn't exactly have a scuffle in the doorway without being a bit conspicuous, so I had to make the best of it.

He said:

"I'm glad we haven't missed this; she's the best *diseuse* in East Finchley."

And I said:

"Lor!" There was nothing else *to* say. So I devoted my attention to the best *diseuse* in East Finchley.

She was a shapeless female in a green velveteen frock, bobbed hair, horn-rimmed spectacles, and a slightly foreign accent, which I couldn't for the moment quite place. She wasn't really reciting—not what I call reciting—she was reading aloud from a limp brown book. I don't honestly think I should have minded so much if it had been a stiff' blue book, but somehow the limpness and brownness seemed to make it worse.

It was all about a little boy. He was being gradually murdered on the other side of an iron door in a bleak castle in Norway—or Denmark—or somewhere in Scandinavia—and his aunt, or cousin, or some female relative, who was on the wrong side of the door, seemed to be rather inclined to go in off the deep end about it.

She kept on saying:

"Oh, Tintagiles, Tintagiles, speak to me, my little Tintagiles!"

And then she did Tintagiles replying—very weak—only about strength one. And so on—for hours.

And Watson said:

"Don't you adore Ibsen?"

And I said:

"Er—of course," and felt frightfully ignorant — because up till then I'd thought it was Maeterlinck.

But I couldn't take my eyes off the woman. She was standing on a little stage—funny little thing—I think it was an orange-box with red baize on it, and footlights—at least, there were two. The stage was so small that it wouldn't hold more than two—and *they* were a pity. I mean, without them it wouldn't have been so frightfully obvious that the poor lady's stockings didn't quite match and that one of them was coming down. Well, perhaps, not exactly ; but it looked very much as though it might, and I wondered what on earth I should do if it did. However, I managed to pull myself together, and had a look round the room.

There didn't seem to be anyone at all like me, as far as one could see, so perhaps my long-haired *alter ego* had got lost in the fog, which was just as well.

Most of the people looked like foreigners. All the women were bobbed, or shingled, or shackled, or poodled, or otherwise unattractive.

If this had happened yesterday instead of three months ago, I shouldn't have been a bit surprised to have seen a woman there with her hair "bargled".

For the benefit of those of you who don't yet know what bargling is, I should explain that it's the very latest thing in hairdressing, and it originated in Bukharest, of all places.

What it means, quite simply, is shaving a large bald patch right on the top of the head, leaving only a straggling fringe of hair all round, just like a monk.

As a matter of fact, the—er—process gets its name from the Romanian word "Barglos", which means "monk", or, perhaps, more literally, "Lay brother". The fashion was started by a leader of society in Bukharest, who, presumably, found herself getting a bit thin on top. So she made a vice of necessity, so to speak, and went the whole hog.

For some reason or other this horrible idea caught on, and now it's spreading across Europe like wildfire.

I haven't actually seen anyone who's been done yet, but the other day a man I know in Vienna sent me a photograph of a "Bar-glee", and it made me feel very ill indeed. It looks so utterly repulsive that it's sure to be all the rage when it does get here. So when you see a notice stuck up in a hairdresser's window: "Bargling done here", you'll know what it means.

To—er—resume. The men at this place were a pretty average set of freaks, too. One of them had a dinner-jacket with a velvet collar, and no one seemed to mind, so you can imagine what they were like. Altogether, they were rather a moth-eaten crowd.

Talking of eating, there were refreshments. Oh, yes! They were on a long table by the wall near where we were standing. They seemed to consist chiefly of cress sandwiches, which had evidently been there for quite a long time; they were curling up and gnashing their cress at you. Fierce-looking things, they were. And water, in great glass jugs. It must have been water—it couldn't have been gin, in such quantities. Besides, no one was having any.

I know it sounds rotten to go to a party and then run it down, especially when you haven't been asked, but really, one couldn't help beginning to feel that there was something rather rum about this one.

I mean, the whole entertainment was, on the face of it, a farce. The green velveteen horror on the orange-box was so bad that—well, if she'd performed at the most primitive penny reading she'd have heard herself walk off. And the fog was quite thick enough to prevent people going to a symphony concert, even if they'd paid for their seats—which is saying quite a lot—and yet, practically all the chairs were full.

I said to myself:

"Why is this preposterous female allowed to go on making the welkin ring?"—or do I mean the Wrekin? No, that's in Shropshire. Obviously, she must be just filling up time until the real show, whatever it might be, began.

It was then that people began to keep looking towards a door on the other side of the room, and "My dear Watson" said':

"I'm afraid the president's a bit late."

And I said:

"What can you expect on a night like this?"

Finally, Tintagiles faded clean out, and the "best *diseuse* in East Finchley" shut her book and stepped off the orange-box—and everyone got up.

Watson said:

"Let's go and say 'how do you do' to the Elder-steins," and I followed him through the giddy throng, wondering how much longer my luck was going to hold. However, it did go on holding—my luck, that is—and we shook hands with a man and woman—evidently our host and hostess—but they were both so busy watching the door that they didn't take the slightest notice of either of us. So we drifted past, and just then the president came in.

Most distinguished-looking old boy, very tall—Elderstein looked a shrimp beside him. Head rather like a lion—you know how a lion does its hair—brushed back and lots of it—well, it was like that. He was wearing several orders. I don't know whether they were really his, or whether he'd just found them in a drawer. Anyway, he'd got 'em on. He rather reminded me of an English duke I once saw in an American film, except that the film bloke wore tight short trousers, and turned his toes in.

Well, everyone crowded respectfully round and some were presented, or whatever you are to a president. The Eldersteins fussed about and talked perfectly appalling French. The president spoke French, too, but he certainly wasn't French. I don't know what he was—at least, I didn't then.

There was apparently going to be no more reciting, for which I was most thankful, and presently a general move was made through the door the president had come in at. We crossed a square entrance hall and went into what was evidently the dining-room.

This was set out, not for a meal, as one might reasonably expect, but for a committee meeting, or conference. There were chairs drawn up round a great long table with a green cloth on it, and sheets of paper and pencils, and so on. And I thought, hooray, this is a meeting of some secret society, and I'm going to be at it.

The president sat down in a big chair at the head of the table, and the rest of us wedged ourselves in anyhow. Then it appeared that we were one chair short. Elderstein, who was doing secretary to the meeting, counted a lot of cards he had in front of him and made them twenty-seven. Then he counted the chairs and made them twenty-seven, and one man standing up.

That seemed to tear it. Elderstein jumped up, very excited, and said some impostor must be in the room. And everyone looked very suspiciously at everyone else. Then the president got up on his hind legs, and said:

"Laties and Shentlemans"(I can't do his accent) -"Ladies and Gentlemen. Let us be quite calm. The proceedings have not started and no harm is done, *nicht wahr*? Will the stranger please stand up?"

Well, I dare say one could have gone on bluffing for some time longer, but it would have meant telling a whole pack of lies, which, of course, I couldn't do. So I stood up and made a little speech; said I'd only come for fun, and apologized for interrupting their meeting—and what did they want done about it?

While I was talking there was a whispered confab going on between the president, Elderstein, and Watson, and when I'd done the president addressed me in his best presidential manner and told me that my intrusion was most unwarrantable and all the rest of it; that it was only a strong resemblance to one of their members which had prevented my being found out long before. Now that I had been un-masked would I kindly withdraw?

Well, of course, I hadn't got a leg to stand on. If they'd been real people I should have felt very much ashamed of myself. But I defy anyone to say they were real people, because—why, because they—they weren't.

I offered to join their blooming society for one consecutive night, because I did so want to know what they were going to do, but they wouldn't let me. So I had to come away—very disappointed—and here it was.

I told this story to several friends, but they were none of them very helpful. Most of them wanted to know what I'd had for dinner. Perhaps someone will kindly tell me. What is this new and intriguing game which one plays at twelve o'clock at night—with a pencil and paper?

Oh!—and I ought to add that the paper was plain—and not ruled in squares.

My Adventure at Chislehurst

TOWARDS THE end of last September I went to the Radio Exhibition at Olympia, and very fine it was, too. I drifted about, and after I'd, so to speak, "done" the ground floor and was going up the stairs to the gallery, I ran into a man I knew. Just at the moment it wouldn't do at all for me to mention his name, so I'll merely call him James, but there's no harm in saying that he was a retired stockbroker and he lived near Chislehurst.

Anyhow, there he was, and he hailed me with glee and insisted on our walking round together. I was rather sorry about this because it's so much more fun wandering about exhibitions by oneself, and not only that, he was evidently starting a bad cold which didn't attract me particularly, but there was no getting out of it without offending him, so I didn't try.

After all, he was by way of being a friend of mine and I'd known him for ages, but we hadn't come across each other for some months, and during this time he'd gone and got married again, unexpected-like. I mean, everyone had come to look on him as a chronic widower, and he'd have probably stopped so if the daughter who kept house for him hadn't got married herself and gone to live in Birmingham. You must excuse these details, but I want you to understand exactly what the position was. At things were, he hadn't seen the catch of running an enormous great house all by himself, so Mrs. James the Second had come to the throne as a matter of course. I had never actually met her, but from all accounts she was a great success.

James was so keen on telling me about how happy he was, and so on, that it was quite a job to make him take any interest in the show, but whenever he did deign to look at or listen to anything he merely said it wasn't a patch on some rotten superhet he'd brought back from the United States. (They'd spent their honeymoon there for some unknown reason.) I naturally wasn't going to stand this sort of thing for long, so I upped and made a few remarks about American superhets which were very well received by adjacent stall-holders. The remarks themselves weren't, perhaps, of general interest, but they landed me with a challenge. This was to dine with him that evening, hear his set, and incidentally, meet his new wife. I hadn't got an excuse ready, so I said that I should be charmed to meet his wife and, incidentally, hear his new set.

It so happened that my car was in dock for two days and James said he'd call for me at home and run me down. The question then arose as to whether I should dress first or take a bag down with me. That doesn't sound important, I know, but it had a good deal to do with something that happened afterwards. As a matter of fact I decided to change at home. I left James at the Exhibition during the afternoon, he duly picked me up at my place at half-past six or thereabouts, and we got down to Chislehurst just before seven.

We were met by the news that Mrs. James wasn't in. She'd apparently taken out her own car during the morning and gone off to see her mother who lived at Worthing and was a bit of an invalid. As this was a thing she'd been in the habit of doing every two or three weeks it was nothing out of the way, but she usually got back earlier.

At all events, pending her return, we went through the hall into the lounge, where people generally sat, and James began mixing cocktails. While he was doing this I had a look round to see how much had been altered under the new management, as one would. The only unfamiliar object in the room seemed to be a large picture hanging over the mantelpiece. I was just strolling across to get a better view (it was getting a bit dark by this time), when James said: "Half a sec," and he switched on some specially arranged lights round the frame which showed it up, properly. Then he said: "What do you think of my wife?"

Well, I looked at it and said: "Gosh! If that's at all like her she must be one of the most beautiful women I've ever seen," and that's saying a lot. The portrait was by quite a well-known man and he'd painted her exactly full face and looking straight at you. You don't often see that because so few people can stand it. The general effect was so realistic that one almost felt one was being introduced and ought to say something. She was fair rather than dark, a little bit Scandinavian in appearance, and I put her down as a shade over thirty.

James finished mixing the cocktails and gave me mine, and then he took his up with him to dress, leaving me sitting in an arm-chair facing the fireplace—and the picture.

He couldn't have got further than the top of the stairs when the telephone bell in the hall rang and he came running down to answer it. It was evidently his wife at the other end, and judging from what he said, she was explaining that she was stuck at Worthing for the night owing to some trouble with the car. Nothing serious.

(He told me afterwards that she'd first of all had a bad puncture and then found that the inner tube of the spare wheel was perished. The delay would have meant her driving part of the way home in the dark, which she didn't like.)

After that the question of his cold cropped up. She must have asked after it because I heard him say it wasn't any better. They talked about it for a bit and then lapsed into the sloppy type of conversation which one sort of expects between newly married people, but which is none the less averagely dull for anyone else to listen to.

It may have been more than averagely dull in this case because it almost sent me off to sleep. It didn't quite, but I got as far as the moment when the sub-conscious side of the brain begins to take control and you sometimes get entirely fantastic ideas. (Either that or you try to hoof the end of the bed off.) Anyhow, if you remember, I was sitting looking at this brightly illuminated picture of Mrs. James. Well, for an incredibly short space of time, I mean, you've no idea how short, the whole character of it seemed to change. Instead of an oil painting in rather vivid colours it suddenly looked like a photograph, or, to be strictly accurate, a photograph as reproduced in a newspaper. Try looking at one through a magnifying glass (not now—sometime), and imagine it to be four feet by three, and you will get the same effect that I did. There was a name printed under this photograph and my eyes certainly read it, but before my mind could take in what it was the illusion was gone and I was wide awake again.

It was all over so quickly that I just said: "Um, that's funny," and didn't pay much attention to it.

When James came in after a lengthy and idiotic good-bye on the telephone I didn't even tell him. He'd have only made some fatuous joke about the strength of his cocktails.

He was full of apologies about his wife not being able to get home and so forth, and he explained what had happened with yards of detail. I'd gathered most of it already but I had to pretend to listen with interest so as to make him think I hadn't heard some of the other things that had been said. He then went up finally to dress and again left me alone with the picture, but although I tried from every angle, both with and without the lights, I couldn't manage to recapture the peculiar "half-tone" effect, neither was I able to remember the name which had appeared underneath. By the way, it is worth noting that if I'd decided to dress at Chislehurst instead of at home I probably shouldn't have been left alone with the picture at all, and got the jim-jams about it.

James came down in due course and we had a most elaborate dinner. He always did things very well and there was no reason why he shouldn't. People with five thousand a year often do.

At the end of dinner we carted our coffee and old brandy into the lounge, and then he introduced me to his unspeakable wireless set. I hadn't spotted it earlier because it was housed in a tall-boy which had always been there.

Needless to say, the tall-boy was far and away the best thing about it. When he switched it on the volume of distorted noise was so appalling that I can't think why the ceiling didn't come down.

There was a long and terrible period during which we could only converse by means of signs, and then to my great relief one of his transformers caught fire and we had to put it out with a soda-water syphon.

By then it was getting on for eleven and I said it was time to go. That, of course, meant a final whisky, and he was just starting on his, which he'd mixed with milk, by the way, when he put it down and said "My word! I shall hear about it if I don't take my aspirin," and he went upstairs to fetch some. He was gone three or four minutes, and when he came down he said he'd had the devil's own hunt, as he couldn't find any of his own and he'd been obliged to bag his wife's last three. These he proceeded to take, and then I really had to go as there was only just time to catch my train, and that was that.

Next morning, during breakfast, there was a ring at the bell, and they came and told me that Inspector Soames of Chislehurst wanted to see me, so I went out and interviewed him.

He seemed quite a decent fellow, and he led off by enquiring how I was. I thanked him and said I was very well indeed. He next wanted to know if I'd slept well, and I told him that I had, but even then he wasn't happy. Was I sure I'd felt no discomfort of any kind during the night? I said: "None whatever, but why this sudden solicitude about my health?"

He then said: "Well, you see, sir, it's like this. Last night you dined with Mr.—er—(well—James, in fact). You left him round about 11 p.m., and he presumably went straight to bed. However, at three o'clock this morning groans were heard coming from his room and when the servants went in they found him lying half in and half out of bed, writhing with pain and partially unconscious. Doctors were immediately called in and they did all they could, but by six o'clock he was dead." Well, this was naturally a great shock to me. It always is when you hear of people whom you know going out suddenly like that, especially when you've seen them alive and well such a little time before.

I asked the Inspector what James had died of, and he said: "Oh, probably some acute form of food poisoning," but it wouldn't be known for certain until after the post-mortem. In the meantime, would I mind telling him everything we had had to eat and drink the night before? Which I did. Actually it was only a check, because he'd already got it all down in his notebook. I dare say he'd been talking to the cook and the maids who'd waited on us. He even knew that I hadn't had any fish, whereas James had, but there was nothing wrong with that as it had all been finished downstairs. I was able to be more helpful in the matter of drinks afterwards, and I didn't forget to mention the final whisky and milk and the three aspirins, all of which he carefully wrote down.

I next enquired after Mrs. James. It had apparently been rather distressing about her. They'd telephoned to Worthing as soon as they'd found how gravely ill James was, and she'd arrived home just as he was dying. No one had had the nous to be on the look-out for her at the front door, and she'd got right up into the room and seen how things were before they could stop her. She had then completely collapsed, which was only natural, and they'd had to carry her to her room and put her to bed. Things were so bad with her that there was talk of a nurse being sent for.

My inspector friend then went away, but he warned me that I should have to appear at the inquest, which would probably be three days later.

I duly turned up but wasn't called. They only took evidence of identification and the proceedings were adjourned for three weeks to await the result of the post-mortem.

I wrote to Mrs. James soon afterwards asking if there was anything I could do, but she sent back a rather vague note about being too ill to see anyone so we didn't meet.

I had another interview with the police after that but they didn't ask me any more questions about food, and when the adjourned inquest came on it was perfectly obvious why. The cause of James's death wasn't food poisoning at all. It was fifty grains of perchloride of mercury. In case you don't know perchloride of mercury is also called corrosive subli-mate (it's used in surgical dressings), and fifty grains taken internally is a pretty hopeless proposition. In fact, according to what the very eminent pathologist person said in the witness-box, it must be about as good for your tummy as molten lead. This great man went on to give it as his opinion that the poison must have been administered not more than eight hours before death had taken place. This was allowing for the milk which would have a retarding influence. As James had died at six in the morning it meant that he must have taken his dose sometime after ten o'clock the previous night. As I had been the last person to see him alive, or at any rate conscious, it made my evidence rather important, especially as it covered the first hour of the material eight.

When my turn came I told the Court almost word for word what I'd told the Inspector, right down to the three aspirins.

The Coroner asked me a whole lot of questions about James's manner and health, and I could only say that he had seemed normal, cheerful, and, bar his cold, healthy.

When they'd done with me, Mrs. James was called, and I was able to see her properly for the first time. She was even better looking than her portrait, and black suited her. One could tell that she had the sympathy of everyone. She would. She was popular in the district, and the court was packed with her friends. The Coroner treated her with the utmost consideration. She said that her relations with her husband had always been of the very best and there had never been the ghost of a disagreement. She also stated that as far as she knew he had no worries, either financial or otherwise, and that he could have had no possible reason for taking his life.

After that the Coroner became even more considerate than ever. One could see what he was after; he clearly had the fact in mind that when a rich man dies in mysterious circumstances there are always plenty of people who seem to think that his widow ought to be hanged "on spec," so, although their evidence was hardly—what shall I say?—germane to the enquiry, witnesses were called who proved, in effect, that she had been at Worthing from lunchtime on the one day right up to four in the morning on the next, and there was no getting away from it. Even the mechanic from the Worthing garage was roped in (in his Sunday clothes). He described the trouble with her tyres and the discussion as to whether she could or could not have got home to Chislehurst before dark.

There was a good deal more evidence of the same kind, and it all went to establish that whatever else had happened, Mrs. James couldn't possibly have murdered her husband, and as it seemed unlikely that he had committed suicide the jury returned an open verdict.

Now what was I to do? On the face of it, and knowing what I did, it was my duty to get up and say something like this: "You'll pardon me, but that woman *did* murder her husband and, if you like, I'll tell you roughly how: She waits till he has a cold coming on and then decides to pay one of her periodical visits to her mother at Worthing. She arranges to get hung up there for the night, but she telephones at dinner-time and, I suggest, makes him promise to take some aspirin and whisky before he goes to bed—a perfectly normal remedy. She naturally takes jolly good care before starting in the morning that there *are* only three tablets of aspirin that he can get at and these are the—er—ones. The bottle they have been in is certainly a danger if the police get hold of it, but they don't get hold of it because she arrives home in plenty of time to change it for another.

"If things had gone entirely right for her, and I hadn't happened to be dining there that evening, no one would have known about James's dose of aspirin at all, but her technique is so sound that I'm able to watch him take it, and talk about it afterwards without it mattering. I don't suppose she liked it, but it didn't do her any appreciable harm. Then again, even if he forgets to take his tablets she runs no risk. She merely has to wait till he gets another cold. In fact the whole thing is cast iron."

Now supposing, for the sake of argument, that I'd got up, and been allowed to say all this, what would have happened?

I should have had to admit straight off that I couldn't produce a scrap of evidence to support any of it, at least not the kind of evidence that would wash with a jury.

There certainly was James's remark: "*I shall hear about it if I don't take my aspirin.*" That satisfied *me* who he expected to hear about it from, but there was only my bare word for it that he'd put it that way, and you know what lawyers are. They mightn't have believed me.

Then again, the Coroner was a doctor. He would have asked me how it was possible to fake up perchloride of mercury to look like aspirin, and I should have had to agree that it wouldn't be at all easy. It happens to be a poison which the general public practically can't get, and even if they could, the tablets in which it is sold are carefully dyed blue. Besides which they aren't the right shape. If you walked into a chemist's and asked him to bleach some of them white and make them to look like aspirin he might easily think it fishy, and I doubt whether you would set his mind at rest by saying that you only wanted them for a joke, or private theatricals.

All of this I knew quite well, having taken the trouble to enquire, but there was another fact which I didn't get to know till afterwards which might have made a difference. It was rather strange. For a certain time during the War the French Army medical people had put up their perchloride of mercury in *white* tablets, not blue, and these did in fact closely resemble the present-day aspirin. Moreover, each tablet contained seventeen grains. Now three seventeens are fifty-one, or almost exactly what James was reckoned to have taken. But all this would have gone for precisely nothing (even if I'd known it and said it), unless any of these convenient tablets could be traced to Mrs. James, and they most definitely couldn't.

The police had searched the house as a matter of routine and analysed every bottle whether empty or full. One might also safely conclude that they had made enquiries at all the chemists where the lady might have dealt. I know they went to mine.

Then there was another thing which made it difficult to accuse Mrs. James, and that was the absence of motive, because the obvious one, money, was practically ruled out. It transpired that she had twelve hundred a year of her own, and the average

woman with as much as that isn't likely to marry and
then murder some wretched man for the sake of
another five thousand. She wouldn't take the troubl
In fact, what with one thing and another, my theor
didn't stand a hope, so I thought I'd let it stew a littl
longer.

The lady left the court without a stain on he
character and later on went to live in the Isle of Wigh
For all I know she is still there, enjoying her twelv
hundred plus five thousand a year, but whether sh
will go on doing it is quite another thing, because:

A short time ago I was just finishing a pipe befor
going to bed, when suddenly, apropos of nothin
there came into my head the name I had seen unde
her picture at the instant it had looked like a phot
graph. It was a somewhat peculiar name and not th
one under which she had married James.

All the same, one doesn't imagine a name for n
reason at all, so I worked it out that at some time o
other I must have actually seen a published phot
graph of Mrs. James, and that staring at the pictur
down at Chislehurst had brought it back to me.

Anyhow, the following day I got my literary agen
to send round to all the newspaper offices in Flee
Street and enquire whether a photograph of anyon
of this name had appeared during the last few year
They all said "No."

However, my agent is of a persevering nature (he
has to be). He went on and tackled the illustrate
weekly papers and he struck oil almost at onc
About eight years ago one of them had apparentl
brought out what it called a "Riviera Supplement
and in it was *the* photograph. I went along an
recognised it immediately, but what interested m
most of all was the paragraph that referred to it. I
said that this Miss What's-her-name had been actin

as companion to an old lady who had a villa at Cannes. One day she, the companion, had gone across into Italy to see her mother who lived at Bordighera and was a bit of an invalid.

For some reason or other she missed the last train back and had to spend the night at Bordighera, but when she did arrive back at Cannes next day she was shocked to find that her employer had poisoned herself during the night.

The paper didn't say what poison the old lady took or how much money she left her companion, but I've found out since and I'll give you two guesses.

H2, etc

I'VE GOT A cat. She's a black Persian—a shocking great beast—and she weighs over fifteen pounds on our kitchen scales, but she's awfully delicate. If she stays out too long in the cold she gets bronchitis and has to be sat up with. So, unless it's really hot weather, we reckon to get her indoors by eleven o'clock.

Well, one night not long ago—it was after eleven—in fact ten past twelve, and we were sort of thinking of bed, when my wife said, "I wonder where Tibbins is." Tibbins is, of course, our cat, and at that time in the evening she ought, according to her schedule, to have been lying in a heap with the dogs in front of the fire.

However, the dogs were there but she wasn't. No one remembered having seen her last, so I made a tour of her usual haunts. She wasn't in her basket by the coke stove down in the scullery, where she generally takes her morning nap, neither was she in hell. Hell is a place at the top of the house where the hot-water cistern is. She often retires there in the afternoon. At all events, I drew a complete blank, so we were finally forced to the conclusion that she wasn't in the house at all, and my wife said, "I'm afraid you'll have to go out and meow for her." So I went out and meowed.

I searched our garden, but as she wasn't there I went through the main garden. Perhaps I'd better explain that all the houses in our road have their own gardens at the back, and these have gates into what we call the main garden. This runs right along behind them, and there's one of these main gardens to every eight houses or so, but they are divided off from each other by the side-turnings which run into our road.

I'm afraid it sounds rather complicated. However, our particular main garden is about a hundred yards long and forty yards wide, and it's quite big enough for a black cat to hide in, as I found. I walked round every blooming bush in it and said, "R-r-r-wow," or words to that effect, in what I considered to be an ingratiating manner, but without any success, and I was just going to chuck my hand in when I saw our Tibbins sitting on the end wall. That is to say, the wall which divides the garden from the road.

She let me sidle quite close, but just as I was going to grab her she jumped down on the far side (the road side). Then she skipped across the road and squeezed through the bars of the gate into the next main garden. I said a few things and climbed over the wall and followed her. Of course, I couldn't squeeze between the bars of the gate so I had to scramble over the top. She very kindly waited while I did this and then moved off just ahead. She frolicked about with her tail in the air, as who should say, "Isn't it fun our going for a walk like this in the moonlight?" and I told her what fun I thought it was. I'd already torn my dinner-jacket getting over the gate, but it's no good being sarcastic to a cat.

She continued to lead me up the garden, darting from tree to tree, until we got half-way along, and then she turned off to the right and went into one of the private gardens. Luckily the gate was open and I didn't have to climb over it. The house it belonged to was all in darkness, of course, but when I got to the middle of the lawn the lights suddenly came on in one of the ground-floor rooms. It had a French window and the blinds were up.

Well, this startled the cat and she let me pick her up, so that was all right, but just as I was turning to come away a little old man appeared at the window. He was so close that he couldn't have helped seeing me if I'd moved, so I stood quite still and held Tibbins up against my shirt front. He was a very old man indeed, rather inclined to dodder, and he had on a dark blue dressing-gown. He'd got something white hanging over his arm, I couldn't quite see what it was, but it looked like a small towel.

Anyway, he peered out for a bit and then he drew the bolts and pushed the window open. He came and stood right outside, and I thought, "He's bound to see me now," but he didn't seem to. After a minute he wandered back into the room again, and sat down and began writing a letter.

By the way, this wasn't exactly a sitting-room. It had more the appearance of a workroom. I mean, there was a large deal table which looked as if it was used for cutting out on, a gas-ring for heating irons, and a sewing-machine, and things like that.

I didn't wait to notice any more. While the old gentleman was busy, me and my cat left.

When I got home my wife had gone to bed. I told her about my adventures and what I'd seen and so on, and she said, "I wonder which house it was." I couldn't tell the number from the back, naturally, but I made a rough guess whereabouts it came and she said, "Oh, then, I think I know the old man. He's usually out in a bath-chair. He doesn't look quite right in his head and he's got asthma or something." And I said, "Well, paddling about the garden won't do his asthma any good. What had we better do?"

It was no use trying to telephone because we didn't know the name of the people or their number in the road, so there was obviously nothing for it but

to go back and see what he was up to and warn hi
family that he'd got loose.

You mustn't think that we spend our lives doin
good deeds, but we both came to the conclusion tha
it wouldn't be nice to go past the house in a week'
time and find a hearse at the door.

At any rate, at perfectly enormous self-sacrifice
went back, over all the walls and gates and what no
and once again fetched up on this precious lawn. Th
windows had been pulled to but the light was on an
I could see in.

The old josser was still sitting at the table, only
couldn't see his face. It was rather funny, he'd go
himself up rather like a member of the Ku Klux Kla
You know, you've seen pictures of them. They wear
sort of tall white head-dress going up to a point wit
two round holes cut out for the eyes. But what he'
got on wasn't a proper head-dress, it was a pillov
case, and there weren't any holes for the eyes.

I wondered for a moment what he was playing a
until I noticed that he'd taken the tube off the ga
ring and shoved it up into the pillow-case. He'
buttoned his dressing-gown round it to keep it fror
falling out.

I said, "Oh, that's it, is it?" and pulled the window
open (they weren't fastened), and I went in an
lugged the pillowcase off his head and turned off th
gas.

He wasn't at all dead, but he'd begun to turr
grey—well, a silvery colour, and I wouldn't have giver
much for him in another ten minutes.

The only treatment that occurred to me was fresl
air in large quantities, so I rolled him up in th
hearthrug and laid him down outside the windov
There was a note on the table addressed to th

coroner, and I wondered whether I ought to do any-thing with it, but decided not to.

Next I went through to the bottom of the stairs and set about rousing the house, and you've no idea what a job that was. If I hadn't wanted them to hear me they'd have been yelling blue murder out of the top windows for the last ten minutes. As it was, I called out loudly several times without any one tak-ing the slightest notice.

I was even looking round for the dinner-gong when a door opened somewhere upstairs and I heard whispering going on. It went on for such a long time that I got annoyed. I said, "Will some one please come down *at once* and not keep me standing here all night." That had an effect. Two middle-aged females appeared. Singularly nasty looking they were, and I loathe boudoir caps at the best of times. They were evidently sisters; I explained who I was and told them that an old gentleman had just done his very best to make away with himself. They said, "Oh dear, oh dear, that's father. How exasperating of him. He's always doing it." And I said, "What are you talking about, 'always doing it,' it's not a thing people usually make a hobby of." (We were out by the window by this time inspecting the culprit.) And they said, "Well, you see, as a matter of fact, it's like this. Father is very old and he suffers from melancholia. Every now and then, when he gets an especially bad fit, he tries to commit suicide like this. We can't stop him because he simply won't be locked in his room. First of all he creeps down here and writes a letter to the coroner" (they'd apparently got several of them), "and then he goes through this performance with the pillow-case and turns on the gas." I said, "Yes, that's all very well, but why doesn't it work? I mean it ought to kill him every time." And they said, "Oh, that's all right, we've thought of that. We always turn the gas off at the main before we go to bed." They had the nerve to tell me that once or twice they'd actually watched through the keyhole and seen it all happen. According to them there was just enough gas left in the pipe to send him off to sleep, and at three or four in the morning he'd wake up and crawl back to bed and forget all about it.

Well, it isn't often that I can't think of anything adequate to say, but I couldn't then. I've never in all my life been so angry with two women at once. It was no use calling them the names I wanted to call them because they wouldn't have understood. I did remark on their unsuitability to be in charge of anyone, and I also threatened to run them in, though I don't quite know what for, but it must be illegal to hazard one's parents like that. Anyway, they got rather haughty. They said there was no need for any one to interfere because they'd already made arrangements to send their father to a home in Kent. I said, "Mind you do," and the subject rather dropped. It was a little difficult to know what to do for the best, because they wouldn't hear of sending for a doctor, and I couldn't make them—you can't, you know. Every moment I was expecting them to disapprove my dictatorial attitude. The patient was recovering, but he still looked as if he wanted fresh air, so we decided to give him a few minutes more.

At the same time it wouldn't have done to let him catch his death of cold, so we covered him up with some more rugs.

After that, by way of something to do, I put the india-rubber tube back on to the gas-ring with the idea of boiling some water for hot bottles. When I'd fixed it I just turned the tap on and off to see if it was working, quite forgetting that there oughtn't to be any gas. But there was—quite a lot. It came out with no end of a hiss; and I said, "Oy, you seem to get a better pressure in this house with the main turned off than we do with it on," and I turned the tap on again. You could hear it all over the room. Upon which one of the ugly sisters said to the other, "Agatha, are you sure you turned it off last thing?" And Agatha naturally was absolutely certain. She distinctly remembered doing it. She began to tell us all her reasons for remembering it so distinctly, but I said, "Why argue when we can go and look?" So we went and looked, in the pantry, and, of course, there it was—full on.

The Diver

'OR SOME reason or other the B.B.C. are always sking me to tell a ghost story—at least, they don't sk me, they tell me I've got to. I say, "What kind of a host story?" and they say, "Any kind you like, so ong as it's a personal experience and perfectly true."

Just like that; and it's cramped my style a bit. Not hat my personal experiences aren't true. Please don't hink that. But it's simply this: that when it comes to upernatural matters my luck hasn't been very good. t isn't that I don't believe in such things on principle, ut I do like to be present when the manifestations ctually occur, instead of just taking other people's ord for them; and, somehow or other, as I've said efore, my luck has not been very good.

Lots of people have tried to convert me. There was ne young woman in particular. She took a lot of rouble about it—quite a lot. She used to dra—take ne to all sorts of parties where they had séances— ou know the kind: table-turning, planchette, and so n—but it wasn't any good. Nothing ever happened vhen I was there. Nothing spiritual, that is. People lways said:

"Ah, my boy, you ought to have been here last ight. The table fairly got up and hit us in the face."

Possibly very wonderful—but, after all, the ground vill do that if you let it.

Well, as I say, they took me to several of these arties, and we used to sit for hours round tables, in dim light, holding hands. That was rather fun ometimes—it depended on who one sat next to—but

apart from that, the nights they took me no manife
tations ever occurred. Planchette wouldn't spell
word, and the table might have been screwed to th
floor. To begin with they used to put it down t
chance, or the conditions not being favourable. Bu
after a time they began to put it down to me—and
thought: "Something will have to be done about i¹
It's never amusing to be looked upon as a sort of Jona]

So I invented a patent table-tapper. It was mad
on the same principle as lazy tongs. You held ɪ
between your knees, and when you squeezed it a littl
mallet shot up (it was really a cotton reel stuck on th
end of a pencil) and it hit the underneath of the tabl
a proper biff. It was worked entirely with the knee
so that I could still hold the hands of the people oɪ
either side of me. And it was a success from the worᶁ
"go".

At the very next séance, as soon as the lights wer
down, I gave just a gentle tap. Our host said:

"Ah, a powerful force is present!" and I gave ₄
louder—ponk! Then he said:

"How do you say 'Yes'?"—and I said:

"Ponk!" Then he said:

"How do you say 'No'?" And I said:

"Ponk, ponk!"

So far so good. Communication established. Theɪ
people began asking questions and I spelt out th
answers. Awful hard work ponking right through th
alphabet, but quite worth it. I'm afraid some of mⱼ
answers made people sit up a bit. They got quitᵉ
nervous as to what was coming next. Needless to saʸ
this was some years ago.

Then some one said:

"Who's going to win the Derby?" (I don't know *wh*
said that) and I laboriously spelt out Signorinettₐ
This was two days before the race. I don't know *wh*

I said Signorinetta, because there were several horses with shorter names, but it just came into my head. The annoying thing was that I didn't take my own tip and back it. You may remember it won at 100 to 1 by I don't know how many lengths—five lengths dividing second and third. However, it's no use crying over the stable door after the horse has spilt the milk, and it has nothing whatever to do with the story.

The amusing thing was that when the séance was over various people came round to me and said:

"*Now* will you believe in spiritualism?" "What more proof do you want?" and so on and so forth. It struck me as rather rich that they should try to convert me with my own false evidence. And I don't mind betting you that if I'd owned up to the whole thing being a spoof, not a soul would have believed me. That's always the way.

I've told you all this to show that I'm not exactly dippy on the subject of spiritualism—at any rate, not the table-turning variety—very largely because it *is* so easy to fake your results.

But when something *genuinely* uncanny comes along—why, then I'm one of the very first to be duly thrilled and mystified and—what not. It's one of those *genuine* cases I want to tell you about. It happened to me personally. But first of all you must know that there's a swimming-bath at my club. Very good swimming-bath, too. Deep at one end and shallow at the other. There's a sort of hall-place adjoining it, and in this hall there's a sandwich bar—very popular. It's much cheaper than lunching upstairs. Quite a lot of people seem to gravitate down there—especially towards the end of the month. Everything's quite informal. You just go to the counter and snatch what you want and take it to a table and eat it. Then when you've done, you go and tell George what you've had.

George runs the show, and he says "one-and-ninepence," or whatever it is, and that's that.

Personally, I usually go to a table in a little recess close to the edge of the swimming-bath itself. You have to go down a few steps to get to it. But you are rather out of the turmoil and not so likely to get anything spilt over you. It's quite dangerous sometimes, people darting in and out like a lot of sharks—which reminds me: a member once wrote in to the secretary complaining that the place wasn't safe—I shan't say who it was, but you'd know his name if I told you; I managed to get hold of a copy of his letter. This is what he says, speaking of the sandwich bar:

"I once saw an enormous shark, at least five feet ten inches long, go up to the counter and seize a sausage roll—itself nearly four inches long—and take it away to devour it. When he had bitten off the end, which he did with a single snap of his powerful jaws, he found that it was empty. The sausage, which ought to have been inside, had completely vanished. It had been stolen by another shark even more voracious and ferocious than himself.

"Never shall I forget the awful spectacle of the baffled and impotent rage of this fearful monster. He went back to the counter, taking the empty sarcophagus with him, and said: 'George, I have been stung!'

"In order to avoid such scenes of unparalleled and revolting cruelty"—after that he is rather inclined to exaggerate, so I shan't read any more—I usually go late, when the rush is over and it's fairly quiet. People come and practise diving, and sometimes they are worth watching—and sometimes not.

That's the sort of place it is, and if you know of anywhere less likely to be haunted I should like to see it. Very well, then.

One day I was just finishing lunch when there was a splash. I was reading a letter and didn't look up at once, but when I did I was rather surprised to see no ripples on the water, and no one swimming about, so I went on with my letter and didn't think any more about it. That was all that happened that day.

Two or three weeks later, at about the same time, I was again finishing lunch, and there was another splash. This time I looked up almost at once and saw the ripples, and it struck me *then* that it must have been an extraordinarily clean dive, considering that whoever it was must have gone in off the top. One could tell that from where the ripples were—well out in the middle. So I waited for him to come up. But he didn't come up. Then I thought that he must be doing a length under water, and I got up and went to the edge of the bath to watch for him. But still he didn't come up and I got a bit worried. He might have bumped his head on the bottom, or fainted, or anything, and I saw myself having to go in after him with all my clothes on.

I sprinted right round the bath, but there was undoubtedly no one in it. The attendant came out of one of the dressing-rooms and evidently thought I'd gone cracked, so I went to the weighing-machine and weighed myself—eleven stone eight—but I don't think he believed me.

That was the second incident. The third came about a fortnight later. This time I saw the whole thing quite clearly. I was sitting at my usual table and I saw a man climbing up the ladder leading to the top diving-board. When he got up there he came out/to the extreme end of the plank and stood for a few seconds rubbing his chest and so on—like people often do.

He was rather tall and muscular—dark, with a small moustache—but what particularly caught my eye was a great big scar he had. It was about nine inches long and it reached down from his left shoulder towards the middle of his chest. It looked like a bad gash with a bayonet. It must have hurt quite a lot when it was done.

I don't know why I took so much notice of him, but I just did, that's all. And, funnily enough, he seemed to be just as much interested in me as I was in him. He gave me a most meaning look. I didn't know what it meant, but it was undoubtedly a meaning look.

As soon as he saw that he'd got me watching him he dived in, and it was the most gorgeous dive I've ever seen. Hardly any noise or splash—just a gentle sort of plop as though he'd gone into oil rather than water—and the ripples died away almost at once. I thought, if only he'll do that a few more times it'll teach me a lot, and I waited for him to come up—and waited—and waited—but not a sign.

I went to the edge of the bath, and then I walked right round it. But, bar the water, it was perfectly empty. However, to make absolutely certain—I mean that he couldn't have got out without my seeing him—I dug out the attendant and satisfied myself that no towels and—er—costumes had been given out since twelve o'clock—it was then half-past two—and he, the attendant, he'd actually seen the last man leave.

The thing was getting quite serious. My scarred friend couldn't have melted away in the water, nor could he have dived slap through the bottom of the bath—at least, not without leaving some sort of a mark. So it was obvious that either the man had been a ghost, which was absurd—who's ever heard of a ghost in a swimming-bath?—I mean the idea's too tterly—er—wet for anything—or that there was omething wrong with the light lager I was having for unch.

I went back to my table and found I'd hardly begun it, and in any case let me tell you it was *such* ight lager that a gallon of it wouldn't have hurt a child of six—and—I'm *not* a child of six. So I ruled hat out, and decided to wait and see if it happened again. It wouldn't have done to say anything about it. One's friends are apt to be a bit flippant when you tell m things like that. However, I made a point of sitting at the same table for weeks and weeks afterwards, but old stick-in-the-mud didn't show up again.

A good long time after this—it must have been eighteen months or more—I got an invitation to dine with some people called Pringle. They were old friends of mine, but I hadn't seen them for a long time because they'd mostly lived in Mexico, and one rather loses touch with people at that distance. Anyway, they were going back there in a few days, and this was a sort of farewell dinner.

They'd given up their flat and were staying at an hotel. They'd got another man dining with them. His name was Melhuish, and he was, with one exception, the most offensive blighter I've ever come across. Do you know those people who open their mouths to contradict what you are going to say before you've even begun to say it? Well, he did that, among other things. It was rather difficult to be entirely civil to him. He was travelling back to Mexico with the Pringles, as he'd got the job of manager to one of their properties. Something to do with oil, but I didn't quite grasp what, my mind was so taken up with trying to remember where on earth I'd seen the man before.

Of course *you* all know. You know he was the man who dived into the swimming-bath. It sticks out

about a mile, naturally; but I'd only seen him onc
before in a bad light, and it took me till half-wa
through the fish to place him. Then it came back wit
a rush, and my interest in him became very lively. H
was an American, and he'd come over to England tw
months before, looking for a job—so he said. I aske
him why he'd left America, and he didn't hear; but
did seem fairly certain that he'd never been in Europ
before. So when we got to dessert I proceeded to dro
my brick.

I said: "Do you mind telling me whether you hav
a scar on your chest like this?" And I described it. Th
Pringles just stared, but Melhuish looked as if h
were going to have a fit. Then he pulled himse
together and said: "Have you ever been in America
And I said: "No, not that I know of." Then he saic
"Well, it's a most extraordinary thing, but I *have* a sca
on my chest," and he went on to explain how he'd gc
it.

Funnily enough, he'd gone in for high diving a lc
when he was younger, and taken any amount c
prizes, and on one occasion he'd found a sharp stak
at the bottom of a river. He gave us full particular
Very messy. But what they all wanted to know wa
how the—how I knew anything about it. Of course, i
was a great temptation to tell 'em, but they'd onl
have thought I'd gone off my rocker, so I started .
hare about perhaps having seen a photograph of hi
swimming-club in some newspaper or other. The
caught on to that idea quite well, so I left them to it.

The whole thing was by way of being rather .
problem, and it kept me awake that night. Withou
being up in such matters, it did occur to me that i
might be a warning of some kind. Is it likely that an
one—even a ghost—would take the trouble to com
all the way from America simply to show me how we

he could dive? Of course not, and I sort of thought that a man who was in the habit of going in off the deep end and *not* coming up again was no fit travelling companion for any friends of mine. I'm not superstitious, goodness knows! Of course, I don't walk under ladders, or light three matches with one cigarette, or any of those things, but that's because they're unlucky—not because I'm superstitious.

Anyhow, in case the Pringles might be, I went round next day and saw them. At least, I saw her—he was out—and told her all about the apparition at the club, and so on. That did it. She fairly went off pop. It was a portent, a direct intervention of Providence; nothing would induce her to travel with Melhuish after what she'd heard—and all the rest of it.

I left her to carry on the good work. I don't know how she managed it, but the fact remains that the Pringles did *not* start for Mexico, as arranged, and Melhuish did.

And now you are expecting me to say that the ship in which he sailed was never heard of again. But that wouldn't be strictly true. He got to the other side all right. But the train in which he was travelling through Mexico had to cross a bridge over a river. A steel bridge, it was. Now some months previously there'd been a slight scrap between two local bands of brigands, in the course of which the bridge had been blown up.

When the quarrel was patched up the bridge was patched up, too, but not with the meticulous care it might have been. The result was that in the daytime, when the sun was hot and the steelwork fully expanded, it was a perfectly good bridge, but at night, when it was cold and the girders had shrunk a bit—well, it didn't always quite meet in the middle.

It so happened that the train in question tried to cross this wretched bridge at the very moment when it was having rather a job to make both ends meet- and it simply couldn't bear it. The middle span carried away and the engine and two carriages crashed through into the river, and fourteen people were killed. It was very sad about thirteen of them but the fourteenth was Mr. Melhuish.

There must be a moral to this story, if I could only think of it; but I can't, so perhaps some of you can help me by suggesting one...

The Hair

I'M GOING TO give you an account of certain occurrences. I shan't attempt to explain them because they're quite beyond me. When you've heard all the facts, some of you may be able to offer suggestions. You must forgive me for going into a certain amount of detail. When you don't understand what you're talking about it's so difficult to know what to leave out.

This business began in the dark ages, before there was any broadcasting. In fact, in 1921.

I'd been staying the week-end with a friend of mine who lives about fifteen miles out of Bristol.

There was another man stopping there, too, who lived at Dawlish. Well, on the Monday morning our host drove us into Bristol in time for the Dawlish man to catch his train, which left a good deal earlier than the London one. Of course, if old Einstein had done his job properly, we could both have gone by the same train. As it was, I had over half an hour to wait. Talking of Einstein, wouldn't it be almost worth while dying young so as to hear what Euclid says to him when they meet—wherever it is?

There was a funny little old sort of curiosity shop in one of the streets I went down, and I stopped to look in the window. Right at the back, on a shelf, was a round brass box, not unlike a powder-box in shape, and it rather took my fancy. I don't know why—perhaps it was because I'd never seen anything quite like it before. That must be why some women buy some hats.

Anyway, the shop window was so dirty that you could hardly see through it, so I went inside to have a closer look. An incredibly old man came out of the back regions and told me all he knew about the box, which wasn't very much. It was fairly heavy, made of brass, round, four inches high, and about three inches in diameter. There was something inside it, which we could hear when we shook it, but no one had ever been able to get the lid off. He'd bought it from a sailor some years before, but couldn't say in the least what part of the world it came from.

"What about fifteen bob?"

I offered him ten, and he took it very quickly, and then I had to sprint back to the station to catch my train. When I got home I took the box up into my workshop and had a proper look at it. It was extremely primitive as regards work, and had evidently been made by hand, and not on a lathe. Also, there had been something engraved on the lid, but it had been taken off with a file. Next job was to get the lid off without doing any damage to it. It was a good deal more than hand tight, and no ordinary methods were any good. I stood it lid downwards for a week in a dish of glycerine as a start, and then made two brass collars, one for the box and one for the lid. At the-end of the week I bolted the collars on, fixed the box in the vice and tried tapping the lid round with a hammer—but it wouldn't start. Then, I tried it the other way and it went at once. That explained why no one had ever been able to unscrew it—it had a left-handed thread on it. Rather a dirty trick—especially to go and do it all those years before.

Well, here it was, unscrewing very sweetly, and I began to feel quite like Howard Carter, wondering what I was going to find. It might go off bang, or jump out and hit me in the face. However, nothing exciting happened when the lid came off. In fact, the box only seemed to be half-full of dust, but at the bottom was a curled-up plait of hair. When straightened out, it was about nine inches long and nearly as thick as a pencil. I unplaited a short length, and found it consisted of some hundreds of very fine hairs, but in such a filthy state (I shoved them under the microscope) that there was nothing much to be seen. So I thought I'd clean them. You may as well know the process—first of all a bath of dilute hydrochloric acid to get the grease off, then a solution of washing soda to remove the acid. Then a washing in distilled water, then a bath of alcohol to get rid of any traces of water, and a final rinsing in ether to top off with.

Just as I took it out of the ether they called me down to the telephone, so I shoved it down on the first clean thing which came handy, namely, a piece of white cardboard, and went downstairs. When I examined the plait later on, the only thing of interest that came to light was the fact that the hairs had all apparently belonged to several different women. The colours ranged from jet-black, through brown, red, and gold, right up to pure white. None of the hair was dyed, which proved how very old it was. I showed it to one or two people, but they didn't seem very enthusiastic, so I put it, and its box, in a little corner cupboard we have, and forgot all about it.

Then the first strange coincidence happened.

About ten days later a pal of mine called Matthews came into the club with a bandage across his forehead. People naturally asked him what was the matter, and he said he didn't know, and what's more the doctor didn't know. He'd suddenly flopped down on his drawing-room floor, in the middle of tea, and lain like a log. His wife was in a fearful stew, of course, and telephoned for the doctor. However, Matthews

came round at the end of about five minutes, and sa
up and asked what had hit him. When the docto
blew in a few minutes later he was pretty well all righ
again except for a good deal of pain in his forehea
The doctor couldn't find anything the matter except
red mark which was beginning to show on the ski
just where the pain was.

Well, this mark got clearer and clearer, until i
looked just like a blow from a stick. Next day it wa
about the same, except that a big bruise had come u
all round the mark. After that it got gradually bette
Matthews took the bandage off and showed it me a
the club, and there was nothing much more than
bruise with a curved red line down the middle of i
like the track of a red-hot worm.

They'd decided that he'd had an attack of gidd
ness and must somehow have bumped his head ir
falling. And that was that.

About a month later, my wife said to me: "W
really must tidy your workshop!" And I said: "Mus
we?" And she said: "Yes, it's a disgrace." So up w
went.

Tidying my workshop consists of putting the tool
back in their racks, and of my wife wanting to throv
away things she finds on the floor, and me saying
"Oh, no, I could use that for so and so."

The first thing we came across was the piece o
white cardboard I'd used to put the plait of hair or
while I'd run to the telephone that day.

When we came to look at the other side we foun
it was a flashlight photograph of a dinner I'd been a
You know what happens. Just before the speeches
lot of blighters come in with a camera and some pole
with tin trays on the top, and someone says: "Will th
chairman please stand?" and he's helped to his fee
Then there's a blinding flash and the room's full o

smoke, and the blighters go out again. Later on a man comes round with proofs, and if you are very weak—or near the chairman—you order one print.

Well, this dinner had been the worshipful company of skate-fasteners or something, and I'd gone as the guest of the same bloke Matthews I've already been telling you about, and we'd sat "side by each," as the saying is. My wife was looking at the photograph, and she said: "What's that mark on Mr. Matthews's forehead?" And I looked—and there, sure enough, was the exact mark that he'd come into the club with a month before. The curious part being, of course, that the photograph had been taken at least six months before he'd had the funny attack which caused the mark. Now, then—on the back of the photograph, when we examined it, was a faint brown line. This was evidently left by the plait of hair when I'd pinned it out to dry, and it had soaked through and caused the mark on Matthews's face. I checked it by shoving a needle right through the cardboard. Of course, this looked like a very strange coincidence, on the face of it. I don't know what your experience of coincidences is—but mine is that they usually aren't. Anyway, I took the trouble to trace out the times, and I finally established, beyond a shadow of a doubt, that I had pinned the hair out on the photograph between four and a quarter-past on a particular day, and that Matthews had had his funny attack on the same day at about a quarter-past four. That was something *like* a coincidence. Next, the idea came to me to try it again. Not on poor old Matthews, obviously—he'd already had some—and, besides, he was a friend of mine. I know perfectly well that we are told to be kind to our enemies, and so on—in fact, I do quite a lot of that—but when it comes to trying an experiment of this kind—even if the chances are a million to one against it being a success, I mean having any result—one naturally chooses an enemy rather than a friend. I looked round for a suitable—victim—someone who wouldn't be missed much in case there happened to be another coincidence. The individual on whom my choice fell was the nurse next door.

We can see into their garden from our bathroom window—and we'd often noticed the rotten way she treated the child she had charge of when she thought no one was looking. Nothing one could definitely complain about—you know what a thankless job it is to butt into your neighbour's affairs—but she was systematically unkind, and we hated the sight of her. Another thing—when she first came she used to lean over the garden wall and sneak our roses—at least, she didn't even do that—she used to pull them off their stalks and let them drop—I soon stopped that. I fitted up some little arrangements of fish-hooks round some of the most accessible roses and anchored them to the ground with wires. There was Hell-and-Tommy the next morning, and she had her hand done up in bandages for a week.

Altogether she was just the person for my experiment. The first thing was to get a photograph of her, so the next sunny morning, when she was in the garden, I made a noise like an aeroplane out of the bathroom window to make her look up, and got her nicely. As soon as the first print was dry, about eleven o'clock the same night, I fastened the plait of hair across the forehead with two pins—feeling extremely foolish, as one would, of course, doing an idiotic thing like that—and put it away in a drawer in my workshop. The evening of the next day, when I got home, my wife met me and said: "What do you think—the nurse next door was found dead in bed this morning." And she went on to say that the people were quite upset about it, and there was going to be an inquest, and all the rest of it. I tell you, you could have knocked me down with a brick. I said: "No, not really; what did she die of?" You must understand that my lady wife didn't know anything about the experiment. She'd never have let me try it. She's rather superstitious—in spite of living with me. As soon as I could I sneaked up to the workshop drawer and got out the photograph, and—I know you won't believe me, but it doesn't make any difference—when I unpinned the plait of hair and took it off there was a clearly-marked brown stain right across the nurse's forehead. I tell you, that *did* make me sit up, if you like—because that made twice—first Matthews and now—now.

It was rather disturbing, and I know it sounds silly, but I couldn't help feeling to blame in some vague way.

Well, the next thing was the inquest—I attended that, naturally, to know what the poor unfortunate woman had died of. Of course, they brought it in as "death from natural causes", namely several burst blood vessels in the brain; but what puzzled the doctors was what had caused the "natural causes"—also, she had the same sort of mark on her forehead as Matthews had had. They had gone very thoroughly into the theory that she might have been exposed to X-rays—it *did* look a bit like that—but it was more or less proved that she couldn't have been, so they frankly gave it up. Of course, it was all very interesting and entertaining, and I quite enjoyed it, as far as one can enjoy an inquest, but they hadn't cleared up the vexed question—did she fall or was she pu— well, had she snuffed it on account of the plait of hair, or had she not? Obviously the matter couldn't be allowed to rest there—it was much too thrilling. So I looked about for someone else to try it on and decided that a man who lived in the house opposite would do beautifully. He wasn't as bad as the nurse because he wasn't cruel—at least, not intentionally—he played the fiddle—so I decided not to kill him more than I could help.

The photograph was rather a bother, because he didn't go out much. You've no idea how difficult it is to get a decent full-face photograph of a man who knows you by sight without him knowing. However, I managed to get one after a fortnight or so. It was rather small and I had to enlarge it, but it wasn't bad considering. He used to spend most of his evenings up in a top room practising, double stopping and what-not—so after dinner I went up to my workshop window, which overlooks his, and waited for him to begin. Then, when he'd really warmed up to his job, I just touched the plait across the photograph—not hard, but—well, like you do when you are testing a bit of twin flex to find out which wire is which, you touch the ends across an accumulator or an H.T. battery. Quite indefensible in theory, but invariably done in practice. (Personally, I always use the electric light mains—the required information is so instantly forthcoming.) Well, that's how I touched the photograph with the plait. The first time I did it my bloke played a wrong note. That was nothing, of course, so I did it again more slowly. This time there was no doubt about it. He hastily put down his fiddle and hung out of the window, gasping like a fish for about five minutes. I tell you, I was so surprised that I felt like doing the same.

However, I pulled myself together, and wondered whether one ought to burn the da—er—plait or not. But there seemed too many possibilities in it for hat—so I decided to learn how to use it instead. It would take too long to tell you all about my experiments. They lasted for several months, and I reduced the thing to such an exact science that I could do anything from giving a gnat a headache to killing a man. All this, mind you, at the cost of one man, one woman, lots of wood-lice, and a conscientious objector. You must admit that that's pretty moderate, considering what fun one *could* have had with a discovery of that kind.

Well, it seemed to me that, now the control of my absent treatment had been brought to such a degree of accuracy, it would be rather a pity not to employ it in some practical way. In other words, to make a fortune quickly without undue loss of life.

One could, of course, work steadily through the people one disliked, but it wouldn't bring in anything for some time.

I mean, even if you insure them first you've got to wait a year before they die, or the company won't pay, and in any case it begins to look fishy after you've done it a few times. Then I had my great idea: Why shouldn't my process be applied to horse-racing? All one had to do was to pick some outsider in a race—back it for all you were worth at about 100 to 1, and then see that it didn't get beaten.

The actual operation would be quite simple. One would only have to have a piece of card-board with photographs of all the runners stuck on it—except the one that was to win, of course—and then take up a position giving a good view of the race.

I wasn't proposing to hurt any of the horses in the least. They were only going to get the lightest of touches, just enough to give them a tired feeling, soon after the start. Then, if my horse didn't seem to have the race well in hand near the finish, I could

give one more light treatment to any horse which sti
looked dangerous.

It stood to reason that great care would have to b
taken not to upset the running too much. For i
stance, if all the horses except one fell down, or eve
stopped and began to graze, there would be a chanc
of the race being declared void.

So I had two or three rehearsals. They worke
perfectly. The last one hardly was a rehearsal b
cause I had a tenner on at 33 to 1, just for luck—an
of course, it came off.

However, it wasn't as lucky as it sounds. Jus
outside the entrance to the grandstand there wa
rather a squash and, as I came away I got surroun
ed by four or five men who seemed to be pushing m
about a bit, but it didn't strike me what the game wa
until one of them got his hand into the breast-pocke
of my coat.

Then I naturally made a grab at him and got hin
just above the elbow with both hands, and drove hi
hand still further into my pocket. That naturall
pushed the pocket, with his hand inside it, under m
right arm, and I squeezed it against my ribs for all
was worth.

Now, there was nothing in that pocket but the tes
tube with the plait of hair in it, and the moment
started squeezing it went with a crunch. I'm a bi
hazy about the next minute because my light-fin
gered friend tried to get free, and two of his pal
helped him by bashing me over the head. They wer
quite rough. In fact, they entered so heartily into th
spirit of the thing that they went on doing it until th
police came up and collared them.

You should have seen that hand when it did com
out of my pocket. Cut to pieces, and bits of broke
glass sticking out all over it—like a crimson tips

cake. He was so bad that we made a call at a doctor's on the way to the police station for him to have a small artery tied up. There was a cut on the back of my head that wanted a bit of attention, too. Quite a nice chap, the doctor, but he was my undoing. He was, without doubt, the baldest doctor I've ever seen, though I once saw a balder alderman.

When he'd painted me with iodine, I retrieved the rest of the broken glass and the hair from the bottom of my pocket and asked him if he could give me an empty bottle to put it in. He said: "Certainly," and produced one, and we corked the hair up in it. When I got home, eventually, I looked in the bottle, but apart from a little muddy substance at the bottom it was empty—the plait of hair had melted away. Then I looked at the label on the bottle, and found the name of a much-advertised hair restorer.

Afterword

A. J. Alan is the pseudonym of Leslie H. Lambert (1883-1941) whose stories for the radio have been collected in:

Good Evening, Everyone, Hutchinson (London, 1928)

A.J. Alan's Second Book, Hutchinson (London, 1933)

The Best of A.J. Alan, Richards Press (London, 1954)

The stories are now in public domain and may be freely copied.

This edition is published by Spark Furnace Books, an imprint of Fabled Lands LLP, whose website is www.sparkfurnace.com.

If you have enjoyed the tall tales of Mr A. J. Alan, you may be interested in the *Binscombe Tales* by Mr J. A. Whitbourn, also published by Spark Furnace. We refer you to www.binscombetales.com for further details.

And in the same tradition, though more phantasmagoric still, is *A Minotaur at the Savoy*, a little paperback that collects the correspondence of the Royal Mythological Society for 1901—which was, if the book is to be believed, a very strange year.